Free to Be Me

by

J. D. Webb

Dedication

Every time I finish a novel, I wonder what comes next. But more importantly there are people to thank who have helped in the process of story. People who influenced, made suggestions, or inspired me along the way.

First there's my God who has blessed me way more than I deserve.

Second my sister who has my back and besides offering a shoulder to lean on, gives me vital feedback.

For this book a friend and fan, Tawnya Jackson not only eagerly agreed to lend me her name for the main character but also read each chapter and gave me a thumbs-up to provide impetus to continue. I modeled the character after her.

I miss my soul mate and 53-year partner, Judi, who always let me stand on her tiny shoulders. I am still married to her in my mind. I did it again my love.

To my editor, Ally Robertson, thank you for your gentile and expert guidance down the path of participles that dangle, commas that need to appear or disappear, and words that need to be spellchecked.

To my publisher Wild Rose Press, a community of talented professionals I am proud to call friends.

Saving the best till last, thank you, the reader, for giving me a try. You are the reason I write. I pray that you love my characters and my story.

Chapter 1

June 2023
Tawnya Davitakov didn't see the kick coming. Stars exploded in her head. Trying to duck, she stumbled. Steadying her stance, she extended the knuckle of her fist and savagely punched back. Her left hand drove deep into the man's belly.

He didn't even flinch.

Kreap! Now what?

She feigned weakness, which seemed to be close to an actual feeling. The man stepped forward and Tawnya shoved her freshly manicured nail into his eye, twisting as she did. He yelled and staggered. He slammed both hands to his face, groaning.

She stomped her heel into the inside of the man's knee and when he bent over, she lifted her own knee into his nose, cheering her decision to wear her hiking boots. She felt cartilage crush and blood wet her brand-new jeans. *Well, that's going to be hard to clean.*

She dug out the shiny black 1911 she'd not been able to get to before and smashed it into the back of his exposed head. He dropped to the pavement like the melting wicked witch in the movie.

Taking a deep breath, she searched the pockets of the huge man. At least six three and probably over two hundred pounds. Of course, no ID.

On a New York City street at midnight few people

cluttered the area. And it wasn't the safest part of town either. A refreshing breeze helped evaporate the sweat Tawnya had worked up. She quickly zip tied the man and tugged him into an alley. He'd made no move while she attended to him.

Okay, was he just a creep attacking a lone woman, or was he something else? Her gut told her the latter. After all he'd spoken fluent Russian when he had stopped her.

The KGB's top assassin, Tawnya Davitakov, calmly trotted back to her apartment. Something told her that her past had galloped into her present.

Chapter 2

One Half Hour Later

Tawnya slowed down. She'd jogged away from her attacker and had returned to her hotel intending to grab her go bag and relocate. Hotel gave the building much more credit than it deserved. Flea bag, Hourly Rate Special, and Rust Bucket were better descriptors. She'd been expecting problems. Crap, problems had been her whole life.

Orphaned in Belarus, then thrown into a Russian special school when her athletic and intellectual abilities had revealed themselves. She'd become an Olympic class swimmer, and one of the top agents of the vaunted KGB, Russia's intelligence arm that recently reverted to its original designation from GRU, after completion of an intensive four-year training regimen.

She excelled in various martial arts, languages, English, Spanish and French, and enough studies of college level courses to qualify as a Master in three different subjects. Her college, not an officially licensed and accredited university, turned out Russia's top spies.

Only seven percent of applicants finished. And Tawnya ranked number three in her class. That only because the two males finishing one and two had connections in the hierarchy of Russian oligarchy. She had beaten down both when they assumed she would love to go to bed with them. It had taken number one a month to recover, and he'd need to be very careful taking a leak for the next few weeks.

Tawnya's assignment, her last for her former country, tasked her to infiltrate a prestigious Wall Street firm and eliminate a man who had suddenly stopped laundering Russian funds. She'd been stationed in New York for five months and had become a valued employee at the accounting firm of Baker and Palmer specializing in foreign investment and banking.

Her target, Bill Remington, turned out to be a nice guy. Someone who had taken her under his wing and taught her the ins and outs of the company. A consummate gentleman with a young wife and two adorable kids, seven and nine. She'd never known a true gentleman before. Something deep inside her realized her assassinations were a thing of the past. Missions to forget.

Tawnya became infatuated with anything American. The way anyone could succeed with little effort compared to her experience. Her Russian handlers provided funds for her but not nearly enough to exist in a major city. She'd branched out on her own and totally off the books advised nine clients on the intricacies of stock and bond portfolios.

Mother Russia would be shocked to find her yearly income, beyond what they gave, reached just over two hundred thousand American dollars a year. She finally realized her new life here needed to be permanent. Tawnya would become an American. She'd researched it. A snap as her fellow New Yorkers would say.

She raced up the stairs to her room and skidded to a stop at the door. Something was wrong. The leaf carefully placed when she left had been moved. Opening her door would slide the leaf away from the sill. And there it was. A foot away.

Reaching in her backpack, she removed her handgun. It was small but packed a lethal punch with her choice of ammunition. Slowly turning the handle of the door, she pulled it open, diving inside. Coming to her feet she steadied the barrel in the direction of the man sitting in her desk chair.

"Hello, Tawnya. Good to see you again." Pietor Abramov grinned smugly and held out his empty hands palms up. Pietor—number two in her class.

"What are you doing here?" She glanced around her tiny room. They were alone. The desk, at least that's what the hotel intended when they placed the rickety table against the stained wall, now contained a half empty glass of vodka, her vodka, and the bottle it had come from.

Tanya rose to her feet. Her gun remained steadily zeroed in on Pietor's chest. She raised an eyebrow.

"Come now, what sort of greeting is that for an old friend?" He waved his hands.

"I do not have any old friends. Get out of my room." She motioned to the open door with her gun.

"We need to talk, my dear." Pietor dressed as always, impeccably, in a dark blue suit, tailored white silk shirt, and Italian leather shoes, picked up his glass and held it out. "Perhaps a drink to our glorious past."

"You have a nerve, Pietor. Breaking into my room, drinking my vodka. I should just shoot you and call the police to haul your sorry ass away."

"I don't think Gregor would appreciate it. He sent me to find out what is going on. You have not reported for over two weeks. Seems to me, that is one week overdue. Can you tell me a valid reason?"

"No. I have told him my reporting will be made when I have something to report. We also discussed my plans. This man is difficult to talk to. Gregor wanted me to find out if he could be still useful, before terminating him. I am trying to get him to tell me what is going on. It takes time."

"Come, sit. Have a drink. We'll talk."

"First a question? Did Gregor send someone to attack me?" Her gun hand had not flinched.

"If he did, I do not know of it. I am on my way to an assignment in Texas. Gregor asked me to stop and…just talk."

"How did you find me?"

"Gregor gave your American name. It was easy. Come, sit." He patted the bed next to his chair.

"Here's what you will do. First take out your weapon and throw it on the bed. Very slowly, butt first."

He shrugged and stood. Reaching behind he pulled a pistol from his belt, holding it between his thumb and forefinger. He tossed it onto the bed.

Tawnya walked to the opposite side and picked it up.

"Now the knife."

Pietor grinned. "I would not hurt you, Tawnya."

"Pull it out. Slowly. Remember who was the best shot in our class. You could try to throw it at me, but I move quickly. Now. On the bed."

He did as she asked, and she picked up the knife and returned to the other side of the bed.

"Now we drink, yes?" He reached for the bottle.

Tawnya anticipated his move. As he swung the bottle, she stepped inside the throw and banged her gun into his head. The loud crack caused him to wince. His arm banged into her shoulder dislodging the bottle onto the floor.

Pietor staggered and fell. Not waiting, Tawnya whipped a vicious kick to the other side of his face and the man went limp.

With Pietor's knife she cut the cord to the lamp and used it to bind his feet. Then she zip tied his hands.

For a couple of weeks Tawnya had been planning to leave. She just had not decided where she wanted to go. Now it was time to move. Removing her go bag from the closet, she hurriedly stuffed her few clothes and toiletries inside and left. She had toyed with the idea of killing Pietor, but she did not murder in cold blood, often.

Outside she headed downtown to grab a cab. A ten-block walk, but it was a beautiful night, a bright full moon, traffic scuttling back and forth, people walking about. Americans.

Along the way she field stripped Pietor's gun and deposited the parts in five different disposal bins. Snapping the blade of the knife against the curb, she did the same with it.

Some day she would be an American. If she could get far away. Perhaps Idaho. Pictures from that state had intrigued her. Somewhat like the terrain in her former home. Perhaps it had been the only good thing she remembered about Russia. The mountainous beauty she had loved. It was a happy walk. She was anxious to begin her new life.

Finally, I am free to be me.
****

Pappy Boyington Field, called the jewel of Kootenai County, surrounded on three sides by Hayden, Idaho serves as the airport for Coeur d'Alene. Tawnya had enjoyed the scenery on her flight into Idaho. The mountains, rugged and snow-capped, led to a valley of a city on the water. Coeur d'Alene sported more than fifty lakes of cold blue glacier water.

A quick check of transportation availability revealed Citylink, a bus service between Coeur d'Alene and the airport. For two dollars and fifty cents she purchased an all-day pass allowing her to travel anywhere in the area.

Tawnya's new ID tagged her as Rene Albert. It cost her three thousand dollars from a private account unknown to the KGB. She considered it a worthy investment.

Right away the higher altitude felt comfortable. The air, clear and devoid of city odors, filled her with an irresistible urge to explore and settle in. Avoiding chain motels and hotels she opted for a four-room family-owned bed and breakfast, the Log Inn, discovered in an online search, run by Otto Spencer and his wife Sarah. They had retired from Denver and returned home to run a hospitable and clean facility on the outskirts of the city.

Sarah Spencer discovered Rene (Tawnya) spoke fluent French, Sarah's native tongue. From then on, anything Tawnya needed was there in a flash. She even received an invite to a home-cooked dinner that night after she had visited several places at the suggestion of her new friends. This seemed like an answer to her dream. Of course, dreams are always subject to change. But until then she'd enjoy her stay. Her go bag close at hand.

Chapter 3

Matt Pearson landed his Cessna Skyhawk in Coeur d'Alene and taxied to the private plane terminal. His reservation for a two-week stay at an upscale bed and breakfast, included plans to visit the city he and his fiancée had planned for their honeymoon. With her untimely death Matt decided to begin this new phase of his life by honoring their reservation.

He connected with his contact and arranged for servicing his aircraft and then rented a bright red SUV for transport to the lodge. Another item on his to-do list involved fishing in one of the many lakes and rivers in the area. A two-day charter of a fishing boat in Coeur d'Alene, Idaho he hoped would be the highlight of his stay.

A once promising actor and former three-tour marine pilot, Matt was injured on the set of his breakout movie. A premature explosion permanently scarred the left side of his face ending his career. An ironic occurrence since he'd flown several intel missions and secret attacks on Afghanistan terrorist camps and troops. A decorated pilot of stealth aircraft, his enemies had named him Ghost Warrior because they never saw him coming.

Two months ago, Matt had helped a young neighbor boy escape a drug gang. Unfortunately, while he'd succeeded in disrupting the San Diego cartel influence, his fiancée had been brutally murdered by a cartel flunky. Fortunately for everyone else, the man would never harm another human. Matt personally took care of that.

He settled into his room. Normally luxury was not something he sought, but this was a recovery time necessity. He intended to recover from the shock and anguish of the past two years. And pampering dominated the agenda. The spa tub beckoned Matt's indulgence. Although hope of a closure seemed eons away.

However, his exercise routine would not suffer from his break. He located a local gym run by an ex-Navy seal, John Lynde, who was also a martial arts instructor.

Every other day Matt would lift weights, work out on the bag, climb a rope, and put a rowing machine through its paces at his ranch in the Silicon Valley. A routine that would exhaust many college athletes. Then he ran a measured three mile run at four miles an hour, and another mile at full speed. He concentrated on remaining in tip top shape.

Just over five thousand miles away, Gregor Baconovic lit a cigarette and paced. His KGB office in Moscow's Red Square although spacious for the state's premier organization came woefully short of the opulence of Gregor's home office. The billionaire oligarch's dacha on the Moscow Canal where he now marched was a twelve-thousand square foot mansion, including a space more to his liking.

Fifteen hundred square feet of deep carpeted expanse with an open ceiling thirteen feet high, the circular room contained three Russian beechwood bookcases, matching six-foot-wide desk and three leather covered easy chairs. An office deserving of someone of his stature.

"Yuri to say I am disheartened lacks what should I say…anger, rage, no I would say disgust. You promised me that whore would be in Russia two days ago. Why have you so disappointed me?"

The man standing in front of Gregor's desk swallowed.

"Sir, I have my two best men on it. One is even her former teammate. We thought it would be a simple matter."

"Thinking which was obviously insufficient. Stop being a thinker and begin being a trusted retriever. My wolfhound might have been a better choice."

"We are closing in again. I have sent additional help. Three top Spetsnaz commandos are enroute and I have been told two days more will be enough."

"Two days?" Gregor exhaled a cloud of smoke. "It had better be. I have a special job for her." He turned and strolled to his desk. He leaned one hand on top and stared at Yuri for a full minute. Yuri swallowed once more. Suddenly Gregor slapped his desktop. "Bring her back!"

Yuri jumped.

"You don't want to find out what happens if you fail again. Where is she?"

"Idaho." Yuri gasped.

"Idaho? Where is that?"

"The western part of the United States. A state south of Canada."

"Do we have any of our teams close?"

"Sasha's *komanda* is in Montana. They are closest. He is one man short. His number two was injured in a training accident. Broken collarbone. He's being returned home. Three should be enough. They are good men."

"You have sent them? How long to get there?"

"Yes. At most two days. With all their gear, they will have to drive."

"As fast as they can. I want her alive. Wounded if necessary but alive."

"May I ask a question?"

Gregor nodded.

"Why her? Why not just eliminate her?"

Gregor turned and stared out the window. *Why her indeed.* He took another drag of his cigarette, then turned.

"You are my most trusted, Yuri. Not many know about her background, and you will not repeat any of this."

"Of course. I have never betrayed you and I never will."

"Good. Tawnya was an orphan when she was trained in our most important section. Years later I found out her father is still alive and is an important man, someone you would recognize. He's followed her career and reached out to me to be kept informed of any of her assignments."

"My goodness, does Tawnya know of him?"

"No. She believes her parents both died."

"Who is her father?"

"I am sworn to secrecy so I cannot tell you."

"No?"

"He has not yet heard of her defection. I need her back to keep him in my pocket. If I need something, he responds. I can do no wrong in his eyes because I have taken care of his child. So, you see how necessary it is for her to return. Our existence depends on it."

"I will do whatever it takes. Count on it, Gregor."

"Oh, I am, Yuri. I am. Have your team report directly to me."

"Yes, sir." Yuri turned and left.

Gregor slumped down in his chair. He sat staring at the thick file on Tawnya Davitakov. He fervently hoped it would still be active a few days from now.

Chapter 4

"How was sightseeing today?" Sarah Spenser sliced Roma tomatoes for their salads. Her round face seemed to smile at will.

"I loved it. So beautiful here. Mrs. Spenser, why not let me chop the vegetables? I should do something to help." Tawnya held out her hand.

"It's Susan please. How about you fix the salads." Sarah handed her the knife and wiped her hands on a towel thrown over her shoulder, then went to check the oven. All the ingredients lay on the counter. Spinach, onions, mushrooms, tomatoes and shredded cheese.

Smells of fresh vegetables, and baked pork tenderloin permeated the kitchen in the three-story log home. Stainless steel appliances lined the walls of the spacious room. They had no trouble working back-to-back.

"So, your adventure?"

"You are correct. An adventure indeed. The city is unbelievable. Flowers everywhere, so many shops, friendly people. And the scenery, mountains, the smell of pine trees. I could not take it all in."

"We're proud of our city. There's a committee for the flowers and the flags. Everyone works together to keep it a place for people to come and enjoy."

"The shops are quite unique. One for just soap. My goodness I had to leave; the smell almost overcame me."

"Yes, if you can't find what you're looking for, you haven't asked the right local person."

"I was thinking I might like to settle down here. I need to find work soon."

That was certainly critical. Her funds would not last long in a big city. She'd saved a few thousand dollars from her Russian handler and her side business, mostly cash to be able to move it quickly and away from bank records. She'd been planning her escape for a few months.

"What sort of work do you do, Rene?" Tawnya's new identity tagged her as Rene Albert from Hancock, Vermont.

"Accounting, banking, brokering. Anything like that. I worked from home, online."

"Let me check around and see what might be available. We should be able to point you to an opportunity right here."

"How kind. I would be so grateful."

"Hey, is anyone home or do I have to fix myself a peanut butter sandwich for supper?" Otto Spenser called from the hallway.

"You can have peanut butter if you want, old man. We're having pork tenderloin. And it's almost ready."

Otto entered the kitchen and gave his wife a peck on the cheek.

"You know, I was just thinking that pork tenderloin might be a good substitute. Hello, Rene. How are you? I see she put you to work already."

"Just fine, Mr. Spenser, but I offered."

"Now just stop there. It's Otto or as my better half says, old man."

"Okay, Otto it is. Otto and Susan, got it."

"How was your first day here?"

"Just wonderful. Beautiful, and yet…um comfortable. Reminds me of Vermont. The mountains and fresh air. Not like New York at all."

"Shall we eat? I think it's ready to put on the table." Susan flipped off her apron and smoothed the blue floor length cotton dress that swished as she went by.

They ate and discussed possible job opportunities, Tawnya's background with limited details, and the Spenser's move to Coeur d'Alene. Otto, at age sixty-two, had managed a large Denver hotel and then retired to his hometown. The bed and breakfast owners wanted to quit. Otto had loved this old home since childhood. He refurbished and reopened it four years ago and named it the Log Inn.

Tawnya woke the next morning at six a.m. and headed out for a run. She had put on a sweater to combat the cool fifty-two degrees and gentle breeze. Her sweatsuit would keep her warm enough. The app on her phone gave her a route and distance she had set to travel. Four miles. She used one of the three throw-away phones she'd purchased.

Susan indicated that breakfast would be ready at nine a.m. and a second traveler would be there as well.

Today she had an interview with the local bank for a vacant financial analyst position. Not a high paying job but it would give her income while she looked for something more substantial. Her hidden offshore accounts currently topped fifty thousand US dollars. A stock market account under another alias worth around thirty thousand provided another small cushion.

Along her route she found a sushi restaurant she thought she would try that evening. The stay here had relaxed her. Still watchful and aware of her surroundings, she relished the absence of the constant buzz in her ear of her handler.

Always relaying instruction, warnings, edicts from Gregor, and never receiving good news. She was never perfect in their eyes. According to them, her performance inevitably lacked perfection. Well no longer. She was on her own.

Yet she still had a feeling, an inner voice telling her to maintain control, stay vigilant and never be off guard.

Chapter 5

Montana same time

A black SUV sped west on I-90 fervently observing local speed limits.

"Close the window, Akim. It is cold in here." Sasha Ledbedev pleaded.

"No. The smell is killing me. Dima must have swallowed a dead whale to have that odor blast out of his butt. I prefer cold to his stink." Akim spit out the window.

"We have eighteen hundred miles to go, and we will all freeze to death way before then." Sasha checked the weather app on his watch, tapping Akim on the shoulder. "It is freezing outside."

"I demand we make him a vegan the rest of the way." Akim yelled to be heard over the road noise.

"Akim, have you not smelled the fart of a cow? They are vegans." Dima Orlov hunkered down farther, allowing another lethal eruption to escape.

"Close the window, Akim. Or I will put a bullet in your left leg. That way you can still use your right for driving." Sasha held his hand on the Beretta at his belt.

The window slid up and the inside of the car quieted for a few miles. The three-man team had been reassigned from nowhere Montana to travel to nowhere Idaho to capture a woman who had abandoned her mission and disappeared. Well, she may think she had disappeared.

The KGB had pinpointed her location and these three drove west to complete their task.

"Who is this bitch? What is so important to want her caught? Why not just shoot her?" Dima asked the questions on all of their minds.

"I don't know. Gregor has said we will go get her. So, we go. I have been told she is a Spetsnaz. One who efficiently kills her targets. But is just rumors." Sasha exhaled his breath forming a visible cloud of vapor.

"We are Spetsnaz. Why have I never heard of this Tawnya? Is she pretty or does she look like a female Gorbachev?"

"There are no pictures, merely a description. Blue eyes, blonde, five-foot-six and eight and a half stone." Sasha reported.

"Promising anyway. Unless her face resembles a cow," Dima said.

"Dima has been without a woman for too long. That is why he smells so bad. No woman wants to be with him." Akim laughed.

Dima in the seat behind him smacked him on his right ear.

The car swerved a bit and Akim shot him an appropriate Russian salute.

Sasha tried to blank out the byplay between the two. They had been together over a year and a half. His team was one of the most efficient deep cover assets Moscow had in America.

They were working off boredom and inactivity. Their last hit was forty-four days ago. Grabbing this wayward woman would be a new experience for them. That and the return trip to Russia could be just the excitement they all needed.

Sasha reclined the passenger seat and lay back to try to steal additional sleep. Always good to catch up when you can. He had twelve hours before his turn at the wheel. He appreciated American roads that were mostly absent nasty holes to wake him. He soon dreamed of Sofiya back in Moscow.

Chapter 6

Idaho Same Time

Matt Pearson arrived twenty minutes ahead of the scheduled time to meet his guide at the dock in Fernan Village. He'd completed a brisk run through Coeur d'Alene that morning to explore the downtown.

He'd only spotted two other runners. A middle-aged man jogging at a slow steady pace and a blonde woman in a purple jogging suit moving at a fast clip matching his. She had passed him as he rounded a corner heading back to his rented SUV. She'd kept her eyes locked forward, but he noticed a glance in his direction and a frown beginning to form on her lips. Something about her piqued his interest. Not only because she was a beautiful woman, but that she seemed to be appraising him. Like was he a threat or a competitor?

Matt followed half a block behind her. They maintained the same interval for a good mile, circling through town. Then she stopped and stood in front of a clothing shop, seeming to tie her shoe. It was an old tactic. Stop abruptly and turn into a possible adversary. Pretend to tie a shoe. She was checking him out and almost as if she was ready for a confrontation.

He sped past and nodded at her with his best friendly grin. She visibly relaxed as he continued on. She turned and resumed her run in the opposite direction. Matt couldn't hope to know why, but that woman was definitely wary of strangers. He finished his run and got into the car. Strange.

Then he headed to the dock to meet his guide and hopefully enjoy some world class fishing.

Tawnya returned to her room. She closed the door and slouched back on it, breathing deeply to calm herself. The runner following behind her had caused her blood pressure to spike. Obviously athletic, fit, and trim, just like every other male assassin she had ever come in contact with. The long scar on his cheek reeked of danger.

The runner had been trained by the military. She knew it. Every sense she'd developed through the years screamed, watch out for this one. She would remain primed to move in an instant. Her minimal possessions kept packed and easily accessible.

But how could they have traced her here? Even she didn't know where she would end up. The KGB was efficient and had assets everywhere, but they can't read minds.

Can they? No. I look for trouble even when there is none. Just be aware but don't create a situation unless I am sure there is one. Now, to prepare for my interview.

Two hours later she'd found a thrift shop, purchased four blouses, two pairs of jeans that didn't fit too tightly, and a nice pair of black slacks. At a general store she bought socks and underwear. *Now, I am ready.*

The meeting with the bank manager went exactly as Tawnya had hoped. Her background in accounting and Wall Street had the man almost slobbering when she agreed to come to work for them on a trial basis. Tomorrow would be her first day as a loan officer and finance analyst.

Her salary would not be enough to continue her stay at the Log Inn, so she needed to find a place to live. Sarah Spenser had told her about a widow who wanted to rent the upper floor of her house. That afternoon she walked to the two-story home on Ironwood Drive.

The brick paved walk led to a wraparound porch. On the north side, an old-fashioned swing covered with a ruffled blue cushion and a matching blanket draped over the back hung on polished chain links. Two wooden chairs flanked the front door. Gray shingles covered the home with the door and window frames offset in white.

Tawnya rang the doorbell. She heard nothing at first, then light footsteps approached the door. A small face peeked out. Square rimmed glasses flashed in the setting sun.

"Yes?"

"Mrs. Turner? I'm Rene Albert. I think Mrs. Spenser talked to you about me."

"She did. Come on in, Rene." She opened the door and stepped back inside.

The short woman, Tawnya guessed around five foot two, wore a bright red sweater and beige jeans. She also plunked a pistol on the table next to her chair. She turned and motioned for Rene to sit.

"Suppose you're curious about my gun?" She winked and sat in her easy chair.

"I am not a threat to you." Tawnya perched on the edge of the two-person couch.

"Shucks, I know that. I never answer the door without it. You never know anymore. Crazies're everywhere. Criminy, maybe I'm one, too." She giggled.

"It pays to be cautious. I am as well."

"You have a gun?"

"No, but maybe I should have one." Tawnya grinned.

"Don't worry, I got more. My late husband, Charles, was the sheriff of Kootenai County for twenty-three years. The crime rate has worsened here with all the newbies movin' in. I keep my doors locked, and my gun loaded and handy."

"A smart philosophy for sure. I am not afraid of weapons."

The living room Tawnya sat in felt quite cozy. A small fabric couch and matching chair sat along the west wall. Across from them a huge silent TV hung on the east wall, taking up most of it. The room glowed in the light of a gas fired log fireplace under the TV.

Mrs. Turner stared at Tawnya for almost a full minute. Then she winked once more.

"You know how to handle one, don't ya? I think we're gonna get along just fine. Let's go check out your room. Oh and, please call me Lydia." She motioned to a staircase down the hall.

They rose and headed toward the stairway. Family pictures covered both sides with Lydia, Charles and two boys cataloging their growth. Lydia waved at the pictures.

"My boys have left for remote parts of the country. Wayne lives in Arkansas with three of my grand babies. Ronald is in the Marines and his wife and two kids live in Virginia. He's serving in Italy right now. Grandkids are growin' up way too fast."

"I bet you miss them a lot."

"Hardly have had a chance to spoil 'em. That's a grandma's right ya know."

"So I have heard."

Tawnya noticed that despite Lydia's age and the fact she carried an extra twenty or so pounds, she moved spryly, pulling herself up using the banister. They reached a door at the top of the stairs displaying a metal sign proclaimed No Trespassing.

Lydia pointed to the sign.

"That remained up after the boys left for college. My late husband wanted to keep the sign as a reminder. We made sure the room would be ready for them if or when they came back. Here it is." She pushed open the door.

Inside two single beds covered in blankets depicting famous race car drivers rested under a slanted ceiling. The room had ample space. A kitchenette on one side contained a full-sized oven, a dishwasher, and a small refrigerator. A five-drawer wooden dresser with a small TV perched atop, sat next to a walk-in closet on the opposite side. This was more room than any place Tawnya had ever lived.

"So what ya think?" Lydia held up a key ring.

"I think I am in heaven. I am afraid to ask how much is the rent." Tawnya frowned.

"Sarah said you work at the bank. That right?"

"Yes, tomorrow is my first day."

"I know they don't pay much, and this town is not cheap to live in. How about four hundred fifty a month?"

"Miss Lydia, I believe we have made a deal."

"I have rules though. No loud music, parties or drugs. Now drinkin' is allowed as long as you can hold your liquor. Oh by the way, that door over there is a private entrance. You don't look like the stairs will be a problem. I expect the rent at the first of the month.

"I'll leave now and let you get settled in. Good to have someone else in this old house. If you're around about six or so, I'll have some spaghetti cookin' and I always have too much. You're invited." Lydia tapped Tawnya on the arm and winked. "Might just be a bottle a wine sittin' on the table." She laughed. "And another one chillin' in the fridge." She turned and let herself out.

Dinner could have received rave reviews from any New York critic and Tawnya enjoyed the food, conversation, and three glasses of a very nice red wine. Lydia refused Tawnya when she offered to pay extra for the meal.

Tawnya walked back to the Log Inn and enjoyed a restful night's sleep. Susan Spenser seemed truly happy that the job had materialized, and that Tawnya had secured a room at Lydia's.

The next morning Tawnya finished her run and returned to the Log Inn for breakfast. She waved at Susan in the kitchen and entered the dining area.

"You!" The runner she had avoided the day before sat at the small table she had claimed as hers. It put her back to a wall as was her unchanging custom. Keep everyone and everything in front of you. The lessons of her trainer. But she had been so surprised and taken aback she uncharacteristically unleashed her unorthodox greeting.

"Yep, it's me. And who might you be?" The man grinned.

Tawnya looked around. She didn't know whether to confront him or leave. He stood and held out his hand.

"I'm Matt. Nice to meet you…ah?"

She looked at his hand, ignored it and moved across the room to sit at another small table.

Matt awkwardly withdrew his hand. "Have I offended you somehow? If so I'm sorry."

She shook her head. "What are you doing here?" Her body tightened and she prepared to repel any attack. Her previous relaxed status vanished, and her blood rush seemed to be so profound it would not have been surprising to actually hear it pulsing through her veins.

"I have a room here. And I'm having breakfast. I missed you on your run today. Did you have a nice one?"

The gall of this person. Tawnya leaned forward in her chair, tensing her muscles. If he reached for a weapon behind his back, she would be at his throat before he completed his move.

"I ran." She waited to see what his method of attack would be.

"It wasn't as cool as yesterday. Very pleasant." The man sat back against the wall, her wall, looked directly at her and crossed his legs.

"Oh, there you are, Rene. I see you've met Matt." Susan whirled into the room with a tray of food. "Here are the starters for your breakfast. A plate of locally grown fruit, yogurt, and a home-made muffin. And apple juice from a farm near here. The casserole will be done in just a bit. Enjoy."

Susan placed the food on their tables and looked from one to the other, frowning. "Is there a problem?"

"Miss Rene seems upset with me, I think." Matt stabbed a strawberry and took a bite.

"Are you okay, Rene?" Susan asked.

"I am sorry. He reminded me of someone I had an issue with. Excuse me." She sat back a bit and picked up her fork. Not very substantial but at least she had a weapon. She'd killed with less.

Susan retreated to serve her next course.

Tawnya played at the fruit but didn't eat any yet. Her

eyes aimed up and focused on the man, peering at him as she bent her head down to appear to look at her plate. She would not look away for even an instant.

"I'm on a holiday, fishing trip for a couple of weeks. In answer to your question." He spooned some blueberries and yogurt into his mouth. And then he peered out the window.

"Where are you from?" She tried to make the request non-confrontational. Not sure if she succeeded.

"California. I have a place in Silicon Valley."

"What do you do for a living?" She followed up quickly.

"Well, nothing right now. I'm doing some travelling. Visiting places, I've never seen before."

She knew it. Just the answer an assassin would give. She detected no accent but that didn't mean anything at all. KGB assassins came from all over the world. Even America.

She fell silent and ate some of her food, still watching and alert for an attack. She hoped Susan would not get hurt. She liked her.

They ate in silence. Tawnya not taking her eyes off Matt, while Matt read on his Kindle, paying little attention to her.

This assassin is one cool customer. Acts totally uninterested. I am not unattractive, but he seems oblivious. Maybe he is gay. I need to find out for sure what he is doing. Hmmm. My handler always said a direct approach is best.

As Susan worked in the kitchen, Tawnya stood up and approached Matt's table. She leaned down and spoke in his ear in Russian.

"If you are going to kill me, let's do it outside. I

don't want Susan to be injured."

Matt dropped his fork. "I'm sorry. I didn't understand. In English please."

Tawnya straightened and returned to her chair.

"Are you here to kill me? It is a simple question." She squeezed the handle of the serrated knife in her hand.

"Ma'am, I don't know where you got that notion, but I assure you I have no intention to harm you, or anyone else. Live and let live is my motto."

Maybe this man is who he says he is. A true assassin would never meet a potential victim face to face. But what better way to put his target at ease? No, I still need to be careful around this Matt.

"May I ask a question, Rene?" Matt finished his fruit bowl.

"Yes." She nodded.

"What made you think I would do that? I don't remember being mean or threatening to you. Are you in some kind of trouble? Maybe I can help."

"Forget what I said. Is not important."

"Here we go, you two. A breakfast egg casserole. Watch out. The dish is very hot." Susan sat a blue ceramic dish in front of each of them on a padded mat.

"This looks and smells wonderful, Susan." Matt dug his fork into the middle of the dish and blew lightly on the steaming egg delight. "Oh, my that's great. We might have to run twice as far today as normal, right Rene?" He reached for another forkful.

"Yes," Tawnya muttered. She got up and followed Susan into the kitchen.

"You want more coffee, Rene?" Susan frowned at Rene's appearance.

"No. I am moving this morning to Mrs. Turner's

home. I would rather Mr. Matt not know where I will be. I just want to be left alone."

"Is he bothering you? He seems like a nice gentleman."

"I feel uncomfortable around him. Not any reason, just not completely safe, that is all."

"You have my word I won't tell him. Although, if I were thirty years younger and as beautiful as you, I might try to strike up an acquaintance with him. He's a handsome man." She winked.

"I am not looking for a mate and I do not want to begin dating anyone right now. I want to start a new life here. Just me."

"I understand. No worry. You go and he will not learn from me where." She patted Rene's arm. "Now another cup?" She grinned.

"Yes, one more. It is very good." Tawnya turned and headed toward her table.

She stopped as she reached for her chair to sit. On the table next to her juice glass sat two red roses.

"What is this?" She looked at Matt who was grinning.

"A peace offering, ma'am. I seem to have made you angry or upset. That was not my intention. If I have intruded in some way, I hope the flowers will be part of my apology. And I will add I'm truly sorry if I offended you. I assure you it will not happen again."

"I have more coffee for you two." Susan filled their cups and grinned at Rene. "Mr. Pearson asked if he could have a couple of my roses. I said yes. I hope this will ease any bad feelings between you folks. Is there anything else I can get for either of you?"

Matt and Tawnya said no.

Susan turned and headed back to the kitchen.

Tawnya sat stunned. No one had ever given her flowers. Obviously, this was a ploy for the man to put her at ease. But what if he was sincere? No matter. She was going to be gone from here soon anyway.

"Thank you for the gesture. You did nothing to anger me. I am merely cautious. And you pop up when I am running and now at this place. I have no belief in coincidences. And this was definitely one."

Matt laughed. "I see. I am not stalking you. I had only been running and we seemed to be on the same route. I run every day, and you must as well. l changed my route today. I promise we will be taking different routes."

"I appreciate that." Tawnya sipped her coffee and relaxed a bit. At least as much as she ever did.

"You won't see me at all today. I have an all-day fishing trip planned. You have the place all to yourself."

"Actually, I will be checking out after I finish my coffee."

"There you go. No more coincidences will happen. We can part amicably." He sat back and again studied his Kindle.

Tawnya downed the last of her coffee and lifted her purse off the floor where she'd placed it as she sat. She hooked the strap over her shoulder and stood to leave. She hesitated and then picked up the roses.

"Thank you again for the flowers."

"You're welcome. We are at peace." He waved as she climbed the staircase to her room.

Matt had an hour before he was to meet with his guide, so he nodded as Susan held up the coffee pot once more. She came and refilled his cup.

"Seems like a nice girl." Susan hesitated as Matt added honey to his coffee.

"What? Oh, Rene? Yes, I suppose. Seems upset or worried. I don't think I did anything to bother her. Anyway, I'm glad you allowed me to steal your roses."

"Very thoughtful of you. I'm happy it worked out."

"Yeah, I guess it did."

"Well, I have things to do today. Enjoy your fishing."

Matt intended to do just that. But he couldn't help thinking that Rene was a troubled soul. He'd studied Russian at Berkley and wasn't sure he'd translated correctly. He thought she asked if he were going to kill her. Then she came right out and asked exactly that. There was more to Rene than meets the eye. Oh well, not his problem.

My only worry—are the fish are biting today.

Chapter 7

Same Time Two miles away

"What a miserable place" Akim lifted the corner of the lime green blanket on one of the twin beds in Room 112 of the Guiding Light Motel outside of Coeur d'Alene. "Smells like cigarettes, and I hesitate to say what else."

"We will not be staying long. Couple of days at most. So, relax. Get some rest. Do not know about you, but I am glad the eighteen hours in that car is over. Now pick a card for who's sleeping the floor because I do not share my bed."

Sasha dug a deck of cards from his backpack and shuffled them on the tiny desk. He separated the cards into two piles and nodded to Akim."

"Draw. Low card sleeps on the floor."

Akim glanced at Sasha and then, Dima. He shrugged and drew one off the pile on the left. It was a four. "Nuts!"

Dima laughed and slowly drew a card from the pile on the right keeping his eye on Akim. He turned it over. It was a three.

Now it was Akim's turn to laugh. He dove into the bed closest to the door and turned on his side holding his head up with his right arm. "Have a good night's sleep Dima." He made snoring sounds and Dima slapped him in the head.

"Make sure you keep your blanket on tonight, Dima, in case you need to fart again. No way we could sleep with his smell surrounding us."

Dima took off one of his socks and threw it at Akim. "See if that smells better, obnoxious one."

"Knock it off you two. But I agree with Akim about the farting. Plug it up."

Sasha ran his fingers through thick black hair then set up his computer on the desk and put the cards back in their package. He found the motel's Wi-Fi and connected.

"She's still at the same address. Google Maps shows it to be a three-story home. Maybe she has a friend here."

"Will be an easy recovery." Dima searched the closet for an extra blanket and snatched a pillow from Akim's bed. "I'm going to go to sleep. What is our next step?"

Sasha turned from the computer and answered. "Tomorrow early we will check out this house and try to catch her when she does her run. If we miss her there, we'll keep watch and grab her when she goes for a meal. With any luck we can be on the road again tomorrow with our former colleague."

"Another eighteen-hour drive? I am not going to look forward to that. Hah." Dima laid back on his bed.

"No. Gregor is sending a charter plane to Spokane. It will take us east to Albany, New York. There he will have a transport waiting to take us back to Moscow. Now let us rest. Tomorrow, we begin our mission."

At 6:30 the next morning the three men gathered at the motel room door packed and ready for the abduction.

"I am hungry. Why is it we cannot have something to eat?" Akim's deep set brown eyes searched his backpack for a protein bar.

"We must stay under the radar. If we go to a breakfast place people will remember us. We cannot afford that. So, eat some of your packed food."

"Is she still at the same place?" Dima unwrapped his bar and took a bite, crumbs tumbling to the floor.

"Let me check it again." Sasha swiped his phone. "No, she has moved. She seems to be on her run. Early for sure. Let's go check it out."

They piled into the rental and headed downtown. Ten minutes later they spotted her.

"There. That corner over there. Dima you are the best runner. Follow her but not too close. She is not stupid. She'll be watchful."

Dima waited till the woman turned the corner, then he got out and jogged to where she had been last seen. He looked around the corner. About a half block ahead she ran with ease. As Dima jogged behind her, his earbuds buzzed.

"Do you see her?" Sasha asked.

"Following now. She is not slow."

"We will stay one block over. When you have her let us know. I will bring the car."

"I don't think I can catch her. Too fast." Dima's heavy breathing made that clear.

"Okay, we need to see if we can intercept her. Hang on." Sasha sped up and watched for a cross street to approach her.

"She is heading into a park now. Too many trees and paths to choose from. I think we should wait until she gets to the end of her run and take her there." Dima sputtered.

"I agree. Wait at the park entrance. I will pick you

up there."

"Waiting." Dima thankfully sank down on a bench at a bus stop. The car arrived two minutes later, and he climbed in.

"We drive over to the house she was in last night and when she gets there, we grab her." Sasha drove to the house, stopping a block south to wait.

Twenty minutes later Sasha sat up in his seat.

"Looks like she stopped." He studied his phone.

"I do not see her." Akim shifted to gaze out the car windows.

"No. She is not here. Different location, three miles away close to downtown. I don't understand but we will go see." Sasha started the car and pulled out. Because of traffic the drive took ten minutes. He consulted his phone and then looked down the street.

"The house midway down this side on the right. The one with the walk up to it," Sasha said.

"With a swing on the porch?" Akim asked.

"Yes, that is where she is."

"Can not take her here. Too many people around."

The resident of the house next door stood on her porch while her dog did his morning business. Two doors down another homeowner got into a tan SUV and rolled out of his driveway. Too much activity.

They parked under a low hanging oak tree with a perfect view of the house. Fifteen minutes later the woman walked down the driveway beside the home and turned south toward downtown. Even though she was dressed in a knee-length, navy blue skirt, white blouse and navy jacket she began to jog.

"There she goes, Sasha. Do not lose her." Dima pointed toward the runner.

"Relax. I. have her on my screen. Not going to lose her." He eased into traffic and followed. "Can not take her here either, still too many witnesses."

"She disappeared. Where did she go?" Akim tapped Sasha on the arm.

"Went into the Washington State Bank. We will find a parking space and wait." One block over a city lot offered free parking for one hour. They pulled in and sat. Thirty minutes ticked by and still no sign of her. They had been taking turns walking on the street with a view of the bank to see her when she left.

Akim's earbuds crackled.

"Anything yet?" Sasha sat in the car while Dima and Akim patrolled.

"Nothing," Akim replied.

"Same here. Maybe she got a job in there." Dima answered.

"Maybe she rented a safe deposit box and took a nap." Akim offered.

"Not funny, Akim. Keep at it for a few more minutes. I think Dima could be correct that she found a job. If she doesn't show in another twenty minutes, we will head back to the motel. I do not like being so much in the open. People will notice us wandering around."

When the woman failed to appear, they did in fact return to the motel. They spent the day cooped up in the small room getting on each other's nerves.

"If you do that one more time, I will cut out your tongue and make you eat it raw." Dima rested on one of the beds sharpening his knife.

"I have a habit of making noises with my tongue. I am sorry. I will try not to do it again." Akim sat cross-legged on the floor since Sasha had confiscated the remaining bed.

"It is very annoying." Dima brushed his hand through his wayward hair. He could never get it to lay flat. He always seemed to be recovering from an attack of static at the back of his head."

"We are all getting antsy about this, stuck in a tiny room. Try to be less aware of each other's idiosyncrasies." Sasha checked his watch. "It is only one p.m. It could be hours before we find her moving again. Try to nap. You may need the sleep if our mission continues this evening."

Dima had already lain back and done just that.

Sasha had been prophetic. Their target began to move again at five p.m.

"There she goes. Looks like she is heading back to the house we found this morning. We wait to see where she goes next or whether she stays there." Akim noted.

"Aha. Moving back to the downtown area. Okay, get to the car and we find her once more. Then we grab her and head to Spokane." Sasha began stuffing his belongings into his backpack.

"I was enjoying my nap. And no disturbing noises coming from you." Akim slapped Dima on the cheek.

"Be careful, my friend. I do not like someone touching me. I might take your knife away from you and use it to hack off a finger or two."

"Enough! We are going on our mission. We will not fight each other. This woman is skilled, and we will need all our strength and concentration to capture her."

Gathering their gear, they packed it away, now happy to be on the move. They once more piled into the SUV and headed out. The banter turned from irritable to almost playful. The team now focused on locating their prey.

Chapter 8

Downtown Coeur d'Alene

Matt Pearson enjoyed his day on the lake. His guide had known where the fish hid. When he learned that no one was able to eat the beauties he'd caught disappointment threatened to ruin his day. Lead content in the fish still lurked from the runoff of ancient mining companies. Locals had made progress in a massive clean-up effort but caution necessarily restricted usage.

All that fishing had ramped up his desire for a dinner of fish and he guided his SUV to the parking lot of the restaurant he'd spotted on his early morning run yesterday and today. Seaside Gems nestled in a low spot near the river with plenty of parking. By the numerous vehicles flooding the lot, it proved to be a popular destination.

An open spot at the south end of the lot under a well-lit lamppost beckoned to Matt. He pulled in and climbed out. The back of the restaurant contained two overflowing dumpsters and more parked cars. A back door sign indicated that the front entrance was designated for customers. He headed that way.

Tawnya was famished. She'd worked all day at the bank, skipping lunch to learn as much as she could about her new job. And she liked the lady who was retiring and whose job she was taking. Betty intended to move near her grandchildren to help spoil them. At least that is what she said.

At last, maybe she could actually become free. Become an American. We will see. She headed for the portico in front of the restaurant and reached for the handle of the double doors. Someone opened the door for her, and she turned to thank him.

"You! What are you doing here? Are you following me again?" She stood with her hands on her hips, blocking the door and not entering,

"No. I'm going to have dinner. I had no idea you would be here. And if I did, I certainly would have picked a different location." Matt sighed.

"I believe that would be an excellent choice for you. Go." She shooed him away.

"Look we both want to eat. We both chose this place, independently. Let me buy you dinner to make amends. You're going to eat somewhere, why not where you intended, and for free?" Matt still held the door open and motioned her inside.

This person is disturbed, or an extremely clumsy assassin. Although if I eat his dinner I know where he is. Why not? I do not think he would attack in a busy restaurant. A free meal would help until I get my first paycheck.

"I will accept your offer. Not as a date, as an apology only." She stepped inside.

"Believe me, lady. This is no date." Matt followed her in.

They approached the small table with a sign that said "Seating". A young woman with a round face and perfectly penciled eyebrows glanced up from a computer and asked, "How many?"

Matt nodded at her. "Two please."

"Excellent. This way please." The full-length black dress swayed softly as she walked around the edge of the almost full room. Two stuffed marlins mounted on opposite walls stared lifelessly at each other. Soft classical music echoed around the chatter and clanking of silverware on plates.

She stopped at a table for two near the back and away from the kitchen.

"How will this do for you?"

"Fine." Tawnya wrangled her chair out before Matt could do it for her and sat.

To her credit the woman in the black dress did not move those brows.

"Your waiter is Brad. He will be with you momentarily. Enjoy your meal." She turned and swished away.

"Rene, we obviously got off on the wrong foot. I hope this meal will be adequate for my repentance." Matt picked up the menu in front of him and began to search for something to satisfy his craving.

"I thank you for this. It should be adequate." Tawnya glanced at the prices on her menu and immediately breathed a sigh of relief that she was not paying.

"I've been looking forward to this meal all day long. I caught thirteen beautiful fish and was told I could not eat them. Something about the level of lead in the local fish."

"How sad. I hope they do not serve local fish here."

"Good point. We must ask them where they get their seafood." Matt laughed.

A waiter dressed in a shiny black suit, white silk shirt, carrying two water glasses and menus appeared at their table.

"Hello, I'm Brad and I will be your server tonight. What may I get for you to drink?"

"Rene, would you like some wine?" Matt scanned the menu.

"I think I would like some. What do you recommend?"

Brad held up his finger. "Actually, I believe it depends upon the choice of entre. For fish white wine is best. If your entre is shellfish a lighter white is preferable. Something like swordfish or fleshy fish I would recommend Sauvignon Blanc, if a spicy meal is ordered then maybe a sweeter wine perhaps a white port or Riesling. If ordering a meat dish, I can go over those as well."

"Let's decide what we want, and we'll choose our wine then." Matt nodded at him.

"Very good sir. In the meantime, I'll give you a couple of minutes to decide and I'll bring some of our homemade bread to munch on." He did an about face and left.

"You forgot to ask him the source of their fish." She stared at Matt, and it was obvious he could not tell if she was upset or kidding.

"I got a peek in the kitchen as we came in. They were opening a box of imported fish from Seattle, so I think we're safe."

"I think I feel better about eating here." Tawnya nodded.

"You order whatever you like and if you'd like an appetizer or a cocktail feel free." Matt studied his menu.

"The prices tell me that I will be happy for this once in a lifetime meal at Seaside Gems. I could never afford to dine here on my own. Thank you."

"My business ventures left me comfortable. I sold them and also had a substantial inheritance when my parents died, so don't worry."

"I'm sorry for your loss. Was it recent?"

"Now two years. They were killed by a Mexican cartel after getting lost in Northern Mexico. They'd gone on a side trip while on a cruise and the guide they had hired did not know the area as well as he had claimed. My dad was owner and CEO of a software company in California."

"Oh my. How frightening. What business were you in?"

"Financial analyst and broker. Retired at the ripe old age of thirty-three. After my father died, I lost interest in sitting in an office all day. I wanted to get out and explore."

"Have you done that?" She sipped her water.

"Not as much as I want. I had taken up residence in San Diego for a while to recover from the loss. Then while there for a year I met my fiancée. We planned to move to my ranch in California and further her career. She was an excellent artist and sculptor."

"So, you will soon be married?"

"No. Unfortunately she was killed a couple of months ago. Now I plan to fly to various cities we had wanted to visit and try to keep her memory alive and close."

"I had no idea. You have had a lifetime of tragedy in a short time."

"Hey, listen. Here I am spilling my guts out to you, and it must be depressing. I apologize. Again. Seems like I've been doing a lot of saying I'm sorry recently. Let's enjoy our meal. Enough despair for tonight."

"I am not sad. I forgot the word. Sympathetic. Yes, that is it. Sympathetic."

Brad appeared and deposited a basket of still steaming fresh bread and a dish of butter on the table.

"Now may I suggest an appetizer or cocktail or why not both?"

"Rene, what is your pleasure?" Matt asked.

"Perhaps a vodka martini and I believe I will pass on the appetizer."

"I'd like a beer. Do you have a local brew?" Matt turned to Brad.

"We have a wonderful award-winning beer."

"Fine, and I was interested in the prosciutto wrapped asparagus."

"Very good, sir. Coming right up." Brad headed to the bar, a huge parquet topped structure with ten seats off to their left.

"Tell me about yourself. I sense a former resident of Europe. You spoke Russian at breakfast. I had two years of Russian at Berkely. Not very proficient though"

Tawnya sat quietly. What should I say? Certainly not everything, but this man if he is an assassin, is an accomplished actor. And he has been nothing but a gentleman. I will stick to my legend.

"I was born in Belarus and came here as a preteen with my parents. I won a scholarship to Cornell University and got work in a New York brokerage firm. I like you did not enjoy the daily computer desk I was assigned. I had always heard about the wild west and decided to come make a new start. In fact, day before yesterday was my first time west of the Mississippi River."

J. D. Webb

"Ah, another wanderer. I wish you well, Rene."

Brad arrived with drinks. "Your appetizer is being prepared. Will be here shortly."

Matt picked up his beer. "Here's to happy wandering."

They clanked glasses and drank.

"Still, you asked if I were going to kill you. Why would you think that?"

"Is of no importance. Just forget I said anything. We will eat and talk."

"Rene, you seem bothered by something. If there is anything I can do to help, just ask. If I can, I will."

"I appreciate the offer. I do not wish to cause you any concern."

The appetizer arrived. "I brought an extra plate if the lady would like to sample some of yours, sir." Brad placed two plates on the table and the asparagus dish between them,

"I insist, Rene. Please take some."

She took one and tasted it. Her stomach rumbled and she hoped Matt didn't hear it. Her breakfast was good but with no lunch she was starving. And she had never had anything so delicious. Ever.

Chapter 9

Sasha turned into the restaurant parking lot and searched for an empty spot.

"I will have to drive around until something opens up. Dima, you go in and take a seat at the bar. See where she is. Do not get drunk. Akim, I will let you out at the back. Just in case she tries to sneak out. Go."

Dima slipped out of the back seat and entered the portico. Sasha guided the SUV around back and stopped at the back entrance. Akim climbed out and stood off to one side of the door and lit a cigarette. He would appear to be an employee taking a break. Still no empties so Sasha continued to prowl the lot waiting for someone to leave. He tapped his earbuds.

"Can you both hear me?"

"Loud and clear," Akim answered.

"Good here," Dima whispered.

"Report when you have something, Dima."

The woman at the entrance turned to Dima and asked, "How many?".

"Going to the bar." He waved at her and she pointed the way. He took a seat at the end of the bar and studied the mirror reflecting the large dining room. He could see the entire floor and had no trouble locating Tawnya.

"I see her. At a table toward the back. There is a man at the table with her."

"She has a companion? Describe him." Sasha

frowned.

"Taller than her. Maybe six two. I would say probably late thirties, not fat. Looks in good shape. Dark hair. Good looking man."

"Are you in love, Dima?" Akim laughed.

"Shut up, Akim. Dima, are they having a good time? Any sign of nervousness?"

"No. Seem to be enjoying their meal." Dima ordered a vodka from the bar man.

"This complicates things a bit. Was hoping to grab her in the parking lot. Continue to watch. Still a full lot. Do not make a move on her." Sasha clicked off.

Ten minutes later he found a parking place. He backed the SUV in to ensure a quick getaway.

"I am in the front, now parked. Third spot from the entrance driveway. Hold positions. Let me know if anything changes."

Sasha shook his head. He remembered his trainer saying "no matter what your plan is, it will not go according to your plan. Something always happens to change your thinking." Now instead of one woman, there was another person to consider. Was he a threat? Would he try to help if they grabbed Tawnya? Or would he run, as it was not his problem?

****

In spite of her caution, Tawnya was enjoying herself. The food could not have been better. Matt had a way of putting her at ease. Maybe it was the vodka. No. She could hold her own with most drinkers.

Finally, she felt satisfied. Her belly full and even laughed a few times. Something that had not occurred spontaneously for how long, she had no recollection. She could force a laugh and make it sound genuine. Training had perfected that. This Matt seemed to be comfortable with her as well. Then her reverie vanished.

"Rene I'm concerned. I feel you're holding back something. I get the feeling you might be in danger and just don't want to involve me. Please be aware, I can take care of myself. My training in the service was extensive and I continued studying after I left." Matt focused his eyes on her.

She took another drink of her dinner wine. She hesitated not wanting to speak for a moment. Of course, she did not want to involve Matt. He could have no idea what he might be up against. And how would Gregor and his goons find her here? She may have been overly wary of any stranger. But she had to be. Her life depended upon being aware and ready to act.

She sighed. "I was attacked by a man in New York. Actually, two men in two separate incidents. From my past which I will not discuss. I got away and picked this place at random to escape to. When I saw you on the run and then at the bed and breakfast, I thought you were one of them. I think now that you are not after me."

"No, I'm not. I too am trying to escape. Not from anyone, but from my recent past. But I want you to know I consider you a new friend and will do anything I can to assist you."

"Thank you. But you do not know what these people are capable of. They are beasts and will not hesitate to cause harm. I do not want to see you hurt. Let us just finish our meal and go our separate ways. I have a new place to live not far from here and a new job. A fresh start."

They finished their meal and Matt asked if she wanted dessert.

"I could not find a spot to put anything else in. I thank you again for this courtesy."

While Matt waited for the check, Tawnya sipped her after dinner coffee. In mid sip her heart fluttered. A man sat at the bar nursing a drink. She had spotted him when he came in. He paid no attention to her, but her instincts climbed to high alert. He never looked away from the mirror, and although he avoided direct eye contact, he was watching her. She could sense it.

What should I do? Is there another one lurking? She scanned the room slowly. No one else fit her image of one of Gregor's henchmen. There could be another one in the parking area, however.

Her whole being screamed leave. Get out of here. But she needed to avoid doing anything to alert the man.

"Are you okay, Rene?" Matt frowned and sat upright.

"Oh yes. Just tired I think from this exciting day."

Matt scanned the area. His back was to the bar.

"No. Do not look at the bar." She sighed and spoke softly. "There is a man there. He may be one of those chasing me. I cannot be sure, but I am almost positive he is here for me."

"Is he looking at you?"

"No. That is the point. He is doing everything to appear not interested. Is a technique used by those men."

Brad slid a receipt on the table. "Your check, sir. If there's nothing else, you can pay me."

Matt picked up the check and pulled out his wallet. He selected two one-hundred-dollar bills and laid them on top of the bill.

"Brad, you keep the change. Thank you for a great dinner. Where are the restrooms?"

"Right beside the kitchen there's a corridor where both are located. It's been a pleasure, folks." He picked up the bills and receipt and left.

"Rene, we'll casually go toward the restroom. I'll follow you and we can leave by the back door at the end of the hallway. My car, a dark red SUV, is out to the left as you leave, under the big lamppost. Here's the key."

He pushed the fob across the table and pointed. "Punch this button to unlock and the lights will flash. Jump in and lock the doors."

Tawnya picked up the black fob, and they casually got up and then headed for the back. She stopped at the door to the women's room and pretended to search for something in her purse. Matt followed and in his peripheral vision watched the man leave the bar and begin to move toward them.

Matt pushed open the door to the men's room and nodded for Rene to exit.

"They are moving. I am following both." Dima spoke softly. "I will take out the boyfriend. You grab the woman." Dima headed to the men's room door.

"Akim, she is coming out," Sasha yelled.

"I heard. I have been listening."

"Do not let her get away."

"No worry unless she can fly."

Matt entered the restroom. It was empty. He stood at the sink filling it with water and listened. If the man followed Rene, he could hear him. More than likely the guy would come and try to deal with Matt. At least that's what he would do.

Just then the door squeaked open, and a man dressed in jeans and loose-fitting polo shirt walked in. His broad shoulders and muscled arms were attached to a stout frame which screamed military. He headed to the urinals and Matt casually watched in the mirror over the sink. The man pivoted throwing a kidney punch at Matt's left side. If it had landed Matt would have ended up on his knees desperately trying to catch a breath.

Matt slid to his right and caught the punch under his left arm. At the same time, he used the man's forward motion to force him into the sink headfirst. He used a chokehold to push his head into the sink full of water.

The man tried to use his right arm to punch Matt. Matt took the blows mostly on his arm while he kept the man's head in the water. Soon the man lost his desire to fight, and Matt pulled him up before he lost consciousness.

Matt threw the man onto the floor face first. Blood gushed from what Matt thought might be a broken nose and Matt placed his knee across the man's neck.

"Who are you?"

No answer. Not that he was expecting one. The man was desperate to breathe. Matt wanted to get out to Rene, so he picked the man up and ran him headfirst into the nearest urinal. The crack of the man's skull on the porcelain surface told Matt he would not regain consciousness for a good while.

He quickly searched the man and not surprisingly found no ID. He did find some cash, a loaded pistol and a half empty pack of gum. He straightened his clothes, pocketed the money, dumped the weapon in the trash bin and left.

Tawnya rushed out the back door and turned left. Someone grabbed her right arm and began to pull her the other way. She stopped and instead of trying to fight the grip, she moved toward the man. He smiled and she chopped him in the throat. His hands flew to his neck, and he began to gurgle.

Tawnya viciously kicked the man's knee at the joint. His leg immediately collapsed, and he fell to the ground. His other leg splayed on the ground as well and she stomped on the unprotected ankle. The man groaned and rolled into a fetal position.

She flicked the key fob and lights flashed about twenty yards away. She gave the man one last kick to his head and ran to the car. She yanked open the door and dove into the passenger seat, clicking the door locks. The sudden quiet was soothing.

Matt shoved the back door open and looked for Rene. Not there, but a man in obvious discomfort lolled on the ground in front of one of the dumpsters. Looks like Rene has been here. He turned and ran to his car. He heard the locks click open as he reached the hood. He climbed in and she handed him his key.

"Let's get out of here. Not good to have so much activity after a big dinner." Matt grinned.

Rene actually laughed. She didn't appear to be scared or upset. It was like she'd just been on a run. Or some light workout. This woman was not who she said she was. *Time for talk is later. We need to depart.*

Matt steered the SUV out of the parking lot and almost bumped into another SUV careening toward the back. The driver seemed to be screaming inside. Matt couldn't see anyone else in the car.

****

"Someone talk to me!" Sasha screamed. He had heard no one speak after Dima started following the woman. Although there was much grunting, groaning and cries of pain. Obviously, a fight or two happened but he had not been able to talk to Dima or Akim either one.

His SUV sped around the corner of the restaurant parking lot just missing another car pulling out. He spotted Akim alongside a trash container. He slid to a halt and jumped out of the car, his gun in his hand.

"Akim? What happened?"

Akim moaned but could not speak. His arms cradling his left knee, tears streaming down his cheeks. Sasha tried to get the leg to straighten but Akim roughly pushed his hands away. And when he tried to examine the injured ankle, the man fought that effort as well.

He couldn't let Akim just lay there, and a visit to a hospital was out of the question. Sasha saw no one in the area.

"I'm going to put you in the car. Nothing else to do. Hang on it will be painful, but necessary."

He scooped Akim up and as gently as possible laid him in the back hatch. There was no way to make him comfortable. He closed the hatch and entered the back door. He needed to find Dima.

Inside he headed for the dining room. At the door to the men's room, he thought he heard a moan from inside. He pushed open the door and found Dima, lying under a urinal, face down and semi-conscious.

Sasha turned Dima over and stared at his face. Blood oozed from a displaced nose as well as a nasty cut on his forehead. Splashing water on Dima, Sasha slapped his face to try to wake him. He was rousing but not fully awake.

Taking a stream of toilet paper, Sasha wiped much of the blood away and slapped him again. This time Dima's eyes blinked open. He gazed at Sasha and blinked a couple more times.

"Where is that guy?" His words were slurred but understandable.

"No one here. They left. Let us get you up and out of here."

Sasha helped him up and immediately Dima fell back onto the wall. Sasha propped him up.

"Steady. Get your bearings. You think you can walk?"

"Think so." Dima shook his head twice. Blood drops flicked onto the floor and spotted his shirt. He leaned down, then straightened and took a handkerchief out of his pocket. He glanced at the mirror and shuddered. He wiped his face gingerly.

"Better?" Sasha still held him against the wall.

"I will kill him." He stared into Sasha's eyes. "Slowly and painfully."

"Right now, we need to get out of here before someone comes in and calls the police."

"Where's Akim?"

"In the car. Hurt. Let's go."

They stumbled out of the restroom with Sasha helping Dima walk. They got into the SUV and Sasha exited the parking lot.

"Where are we going?" Dima asked. He looked in the back. Akim huddled there in a mass. Every bump the car encountered elicited a grunt of pain from Akim.

"We go back to the motel and take care of you two. Then we meet death."

"What do you mean meet death?" Dima frowned.

"We have a call to make to Gregor. Do you not think he will kill us because we could not catch this woman?"

"She had help. We could not foresee that." Dima held his handkerchief over his head gash.

"What does Gregor say about excuses?"

Dima frowned. "They become reasons for extermination."

On the way to the motel no conversation was necessary. The only sounds were pathetic mutterings and whimpering from Akim.

Chapter 10

"Why should I bring you back to Moscow? Two of you are wounded. What good are you? Besides being a pain in my ass. You seem to collectively have the brain power of one of the big rats running around my barn. No, maybe they are smarter." Gregor Baconovic paced in front of his desk.

"We did not anticipate she would have anyone with her. Especially one who could fight. It looks like she picked up a bodyguard or boyfriend. I patched up Dima and got a boot and crutches for Akim. We can make it back."

"Am I surrounded by incompetents? This is only one woman. Do I have to do it myself? All right. Get to the Spokane airport and get on that plane. It leaves in three hours." He clicked off and threw the phone on his desk.

Gregor sat down in his normally comfortable ergonomic chair and held his head in his hands. It had been nine months since he'd sent Tawnya to New York. It was supposed to be for only three or four months. She had completed many assignments before this one. Usually ahead of the estimated length.

What was different this time? Granted it was New York, her first time assigned in the USA. But she had drawn this one out, missed check-ins and gave vague answers to queries from her contact. Not like her at all.

Maybe she had become attached to her target. Maybe they had become lovers.

Gregor shook his head. No, I do not think so. He remembered how cold she was. Unfeeling. At one point he had wondered if she was a lesbian. Their lovemaking was anything but passionate. But still he had to have her. When he got her back home he could make her a valuable asset again. But first he had to get her here.

"Anya, come here." He got up and stood at his desk.

"Yes, sir?" Anya Vanosic entered and approached.

"Contact Dmitri. I need him here yesterday."

"I heard from him today. He will complete his task by tomorrow."

"Good. Have him select two special forces men. Top performers. The best. I have a new mission for them."

"Spetsnaz?" She raised her eyebrows. He noticed how brown Anya's eyes were. Chocolate brown.

"His choice. Whatever he needs."

Anya Vanosic nodded, gracefully turned and left. She had been his assistant and top handler of KGB assassins. She single-handedly directed the two best men the KGB had and the best woman, Tawnya. A thirty-nine-year-old former instructor for the secret group of terminators called the Wolf Pack. Seven of the most competent and highly trained human weapons who went where there was a need to handle an assassination or create an event that would disrupt or destroy a target identified by the KGB.

A beauty with a sharp face, shiny cheekbones, dark brown hair cut in a pageboy style and a figure that was full and hard to hide even though she tried. Loose clothing was her uniform of the day. She was also happily married, and Gregor was positive she could kill him eleven different ways.

She was so valuable to him he would never make advances toward her. Not that he had not fanaticized about it.

Two days later Dmitri Oborin materialized and was shown into Gregor's office.

"Dmitri, come in, come in. How are you?"

"I am well, sir. A bit tired. I was told to not waste any time getting back. I took that to mean it was important." He stood in front of Gregor's desk in almost stiff attention.

"Sit. Relax. This is not an inquisition." Gregor motioned to a chair. They sat.

"I have not received your report. I assume your mission was successful?

"Most definitely. There was no problem. The man had a serious accident. Unfortunately, he did not survive." Dmitri's face was expressionless.

"Unfortunately. Quite." Gregor shrugged.

"The man's brakes failed, and his car plunged over an embankment. The drop was one hundred ten feet the Swedish authorities told me. Unlike the movies the car did not explode, but it did become a ghost of its former self. And surprisingly the air bag failed to deploy."

"One less impediment. Good."

"What do you have for me?" Dmitri sat back and crossed his legs.

"An interesting situation which I think you might enjoy."

"I enjoy all my assignments."

"Do you remember Tawnya?"

"Oh yes. She and I had a great competition during our training."

"She has become shall we say, a problem."

"How so? I had been impressed with her performance. From what I heard she was almost as good as me." A smirk appeared on Dmitri's face.

"Quite right. Up until a few months ago. We sent her to New York to determine why our operation had stalled. We had been using a firm to stockpile funds and do transfers when necessary. Our contact there quit communicating and completing his tasks. Then the same thing happened with Tawnya."

"Do we know why?"

"No. I sent one man to capture her, and he failed. Then Pietor confronted her, and she slipped away. We located her in Idaho, and I sent Dima, Akim and Sasha to bring her back. They ended up hurt and yesterday they returned home."

"She escaped those three? I know she's good but that is hard to believe."

"Dima has a repaired broken nose and a slight concussion and Akim is having surgery on his left knee and right ankle tomorrow. He will be out of commission for at least six months."

"And Sasha?"

"He is okay. Tawnya had help from an American. We are trying to get information on him. He just showed up."

"You want me to go get her, I assume."

"Yes. Pick two men to take with you. I want no more hindrances. Bring her back. Do not kill her. I want what information she has. As for the American, he needs to find out what happens when you interfere with us. You are good with accidents. Improvise." Gregor stood signaling the meeting was over.

"I will take Sasha because he has seen this American and two more. It will be done."

"Make sure of it. Do not fail." Gregor held up his hand. "Wait a moment. Take one man and stop in New York. Pick up Pietor. He will be anxious to help. She escaped him as well."

"She did? We will do this. You have my word."

Chapter 11

Matt steered the SUV through downtown Coeur d'Alene, keeping an eye on the rearview mirror. No one followed that he could tell. He decided to do a check to make sure. Changing lanes often, then taking a quick turn onto three different side streets. They were clear.

"We need to talk. I mean really talk. You're not telling me the whole story and I can't help if I'm kept in the dark." He glanced at Rene. She'd been quiet since their escape, staring straight ahead.

"I do not want you to get hurt. You seem nice, I am sorry you got mixed up in this." She didn't look at him.

"That's just the point. I am involved. Those men were at the least trying to kidnap you and at the worst trying to kill you. They were Russian. What's the story?"

"Take me home. For right now my temporary home." She sighed. "We will talk."

She directed Matt to Lydia's house.

"Pull into the driveway to the back. There is a rear entrance to my room."

Matt parked and they got out. As they climbed the steps Rene held up her hand.

"Wait here for a bit. I need to check something." She reached the second step from the top and stooped to look at the top step. Then she hopped up on the deck and bent down to examine the doorknob. "Is okay. Do not step on the first step and come up."

"Why not?'

"I have booby trap there. Step on that string of floss and two pots fall from underneath and clang together. Very loud."

Matt shook his head and carefully avoided the dangerous plank.

Rene fiddled with the key, opened her back door and entered.

Matt stepped inside. The uncluttered room, small and neat, featured twin beds under a sloping ceiling.

"I see you're a racing fan. I wouldn't have guessed that." Matt chuckled.

"Is blanket left from Lydia's sons. I had to google that word to see what it meant." She sat on one of the beds and threw her purse down beside her.

Matt turned around a metal chair from under a small kitchen table and sat. They were silent for a few seconds.

"We were going to talk. Your turn." Matt waited.

"I need to leave. Those men will be back." Rene rested her elbows on her knees and looked up at Matt.

"I doubt two of them will be in any shape to come after you soon. You did a number on the guy next to the dumpster. And the one who followed me into the restroom will have difficulty breathing normally for I'd say a week or two. And he suddenly developed a noticeable limp."

"I know you're specially trained. The kind of training I've had. I'd say GRU or KGB or both. You are a Russian operative of some sort. Don't deny it because I won't believe anything else."

Rene remained silent, her facial expression unchanged.

"Since those guys were after you, you either ticked

off some Russian handler or contact, or you're fleeing from someone tied to the Russian mob or government. Either way you're not going to be able to get away by yourself. If I hadn't been there, they would have taken you or left you dead."

Still nothing from Rene.

"I seem to be the only active side of this conversation. Talk. You need help. I can give it to you."

A knock at the door startled them both.

"Rene, it's Lydia. Are you okay? There's a car parked out back. I don't recognize it."

"Is okay, Lydia. A friend."

"Can I come in?"

"Yes, just a minute." Rene got up and let Lydia in.

She had her purse in front of her and when Rene returned to her seat on the bed, Lydia pulled her revolver out and pointed it at Matt.

"Hands where I can see 'em, mister." Her hand didn't quiver even with a heavy revolver in it.

"Lydia, he is okay. I brought him here."

"Just makin' sure, honey. Can't be too careful nowadays. Show me some ID if you don't mind, mister."

Matt eased out his wallet. He offered his license to Lydia.

"Give it to Rene then she can bring it over here."

Rene took the ID and walked over to Lydia. Lydia looked it over and gave it back to Rene.

"So what's the story, Mr. Pearson?"

Rene handed Matt his ID and sat again.

"Lydia, I had a bit of trouble and Matt helped me out and brought me back here. He and I had a misunderstanding and he bought me dinner to apologize."

"A man helping you and apologizing at the same time. Honey don't let this man get away. You confiscate him quick." She eased the hammer down on the pistol and put it into her purse.

"We are merely friends."

"This have anything to do with an altercation at the Seaside Gem?"

"What do you know about that, ma'am?" Matt asked.

"Heard it on the police scanner." She smiled at Matt. "My late husband was a sheriff here and I enjoy listenin' to it. Reports of a possible fight and injuries but when they got there, they didn't find anyone.

"A man reported seeing a car being loaded with a couple of injured guys. However, the hospital had no one show up for treatment. Seems like some damage to a urinal in the bathroom and lots of blood on the floor. No other witnesses came forward. And it seems like you got a bit of scratches on your hand, Matt. And that could be blood on your shoe." She grinned.

"I plead the fifth, Lydia."

"I'd sure like to hear the story someday." She raised her eyebrows.

"Maybe someday." Matt nodded.

"Okay, I'll leave you alone. If ya need anything let me know."

"Lydia, before you go, I have something to tell you. I will be leaving tomorrow. Things just didn't work out for me here. I'm sorry because I like it here."

"Oh, I'm sorry, too. Would have been nice to have a young person around, one who can shake things up a bit."

"What do I owe you?"

"Let's call it fifty bucks and we're good."

Matt was putting his license away and pulled out a fifty-dollar-bill.

"Here you are, Lydia. I just love a gun-toting landlady." He rose and gave her the money.

"You don't have to do that for me, Matt. Please." Rene touched his arm.

"Rene, let him. And like I said, don't let him get away." Lydia waved and left, pulling the door shut.

"Now where were we? Oh yes, you were about to spill the beans." Matt sat in his chair.

"What is spilling the beans?"

"Telling your story."

"I do not know where to begin. And some of it will remain unsaid."

Tawnya was hesitant. Also confused, worried and unsure about everything. She had always been on her own. No one knew her whole story. Gregor had the most knowledge, but even he was clueless on some of her encounters.

One thing she knew, Matt was right about needing help. That, too, was unfamiliar. Was Matt the right one to lean on? He seemed to want to help, and it was a new experience to have someone offer help without wanting something in return.

Right now, her mind was spinning. So many questions, so few answers. Actually, none at the moment. What other options did she have? Again, none. She needed someone American to help guide her. To help her become invisible to the KGB.

"Would you like a drink? I have vodka or soda."

"I'm fine. Still full from dinner."

"Okay. Where to start. My name is not Rene, it is

Tawnya. Tawnya Davitakov. At least that is what name I was assigned. My parents died when I was three. I never knew their names. I went from orphanage to orphanage as I was considered trouble. Rebellious early on.

"Then someone discovered my athletic abilities. Very good swimmer. At a special school when I was thirteen my training became focused. I studied languages, English, Spanish, German, and French. And weapons training began. Rifles, pistols, knives and of course martial arts."

"You were being trained as a spy."

"Yes, I excelled. One of the men who attacked me in New York was second in my class. Pietor Abramov. I left him tied up in my hotel room. I was third in my class." She held up her forefinger. "Only because I am a woman."

"What type of work did you do?"

"It will remain my secret. But I completed every one of my missions. Then about nine months ago I was sent to New York. I became enamored with America. I was tired of my job, and I decided to quit and become an American."

"I am assuming that didn't go over very well with your leadership."

"I would assume that as well. I did not tell them I was leaving. An American would just leave. I consider it my first act of being an American."

"So, you're not here legally?"

"I have identification. Actually, three sets with different names provided by my handler. But no, I am not here officially." She shrugged. "Has never been a problem."

"Well, it will be if you want to become an American.

It will require documentation. At least a green card."

"I have one of those as well." She held up her purse.

"As of right now it's not our major concern. We need to get you away from here."

"This will be my second escape. Somehow, they keep finding me."

Matt sat and thought for a minute.

"Rene, or I guess Tawnya, have you had much surgery done?"

"Oh yes. Appendix and a couple of um, repairs."

"Repairs? What repairs?"

"Two bullet wounds. One to my leg and one just above my hip."

"When?"

"Let me see. My leg was three years ago, and my side was about ten years. Why?"

"That's how they keep locating you. A chip. They planted a tracking chip in you."

"Tracking chip? Yes, it must be. How do we disable it?"

"I'm afraid it will have to come out. It won't be fun. Probably buried an inch or so under the skin."

"I think I know where it is. The scar in my side itches constantly. When I scratch it, it never seems to stop."

"Can you feel anything solid in your side?"

"No, it just itches."

"Do you trust me?"

Tawnya stared at Matt. She did not know how to answer. To a point she trusted Matt, or she wouldn't be telling him her background. But trust? No. Something she had never fully given to anyone.

No one had ever shown her the slightest reason for

trust. Her training had stressed not to trust anyone. Of course, they said except them. But she never trusted either her handlers or her instructors. That by instinct.

"I cannot give you a positive answer. I have only had one person in my life I could say I trusted. My husband. So, I guess I would say a little bit."

"Your husband? Where is he?"

"He died in Syria ten years ago. He was caught in a cloud of serin gas that was blown back on his unit. He and eight others died."

"I'm so sorry."

"Long time ago. I miss him." She concentrated on not showing any sort of grief.

"I propose we take it out. Otherwise, they will always find you. Will also make it easier to become an American."

"You? Can you do this?"

"In the military I had medical training. We had to patch each other up when no medic was available. I've done in field wound repair many times. Even once to myself."

"Okay. I think it best that we, you do it."

"It will hurt. And I don't have any anesthesia."

"Then the quicker we get it done the quicker the pain will be gone."

"I'll get the first aid kit and be right back." Matt got up and headed for his SUV and his backpack. When he returned Tawnya had her shirt lifted off her side and was examining her scar. Apparently hard to see because it was more to her back than in front.

"I'm going to borrow some of your vodka for cleaning the area."

He went into the kitchen and retrieved a bottle. He

also found a pot to boil water to sterilize his knife. From his kit he extracted a pair of needle nose pliers, and a needle. He dropped those into the pan on the stove to heat.

"Now this is what I'm going to do. I have a needle over there which I will use to locate the chip. Then I'll make an incision and remove it." He raised his eyebrows. "You won't have that nasty itch anymore."

"This will be a good thing."

Thirty minutes later the chip had been extracted, cleaned, and placed in a paper towel to dry. Matt had remarked to Tawnya she was one of his best patients ever. She'd cried out only once through gritted teeth. Matt applied clotting material and wrapped her side with gauze.

"There you go. Good as new."

Tawnya picked up the chip and studied it.

"What are we going to do with this thing? Is it still tracking?"

"I was careful not to damage it. Should be working. We're going to attach it to the first truck we can find that is heading east. This we call a wild goose chase in America. Seems only fitting, don't you think?"

Her smile answered his question.

They said goodbye to Lydia and took the SUV back to the bed and breakfast to pick up Matt's belongings and settle his bill. Tawnya sat in the easy chair in Matt's room.

"What now? Where do we go?" She tried to move to a more comfortable position. It seemed like every move she made affected her new wound. Even breathing caused shots of pain. She had suffered worse pain from other instances, so she knew this would be just a minor setback.

"I have a suggestion. It's totally up to you to decide. I'll accept whatever you say. I have a ranch in Silicon Valley. Out of the way, where you can recuperate and give thought to your future. You're welcome there as long as you'd like. No strings, no obligation. I have plenty of room."

"Silicon Valley? Where is this?"

"California near San Francisco. Surrounded by mountains and space."

"Mountains. I like this. Can I go hiking?"

"That is a requirement." Matt laughed. "You must hike, and I can show you the best views. Some so breathtaking that rival any on this planet."

"I will consider it. Do we drive there?"

"No. We fly. I have my own plane."

"You are pilot?"

"Yes."

"Are you a good pilot?" She tilted her head.

"I guess we'll have to see, won't we? If you're coming."

"I need more data. How big is this ranch?"

"One-hundred-ninety-two acres."

"Goodness. That is no ranch. It is a state."

"I told you, plenty of room. There's a water reservoir stocked with game fish, four barns for my horses and equipment. No one will know where you are. You will be safe. What do you say?" Matt zipped up his luggage and set it upright on the floor.

"I only have one last question. Why are you helping me? What is your motive? I can think of no benefit for you. I cannot pay you. I am hunted, wounded, not looking for any attachment. Danger surrounds me. I do not understand."

"My parents instilled in me a need to help when able, how to evaluate a person's intent and value. I determined for myself you are a good person who needs assistance. Until you prove me wrong, I will stand by that and help you become an American."

She struggled a bit but managed to rise. She edged over to him and patted him on his shoulder. "When do we leave?"

Tawnya had never been so touched. This man was so unlike almost every man she had ever met. Yes, she had shed tears before. Mostly from some racking pain she endured. But now her eyes had watered. An unfamiliar emotion hit her like a hammer. She was grateful to Matt and instinctively knew she would never be able to let him know the depth of that feeling.

Could she really be free? Her decisions, plans, desires all under her control. She wanted to shout, to let this surface. This is what it means to be free.

Then her training instructor's words pushed their way forward. A giant of a man who loved inflicting pain. He often picked Tawnya to be his teaching tool. His gravelly voice became almost audible. "When everything appears to be perfect and no more worries are present, that is when everything goes to hell."

On the way to the airport, they stopped at a huge truck plaza populated by several long-haul trucks and Matt got out.

"I'm going to attach this tracker to a truck. Should throw them off our trail. Give me about ten minutes to find one going far enough away." He gave her a thumbs up and she returned the gesture.

When Matt returned in a few minutes, he had a big

grin on his face.

"Why do you laugh?"

"I happened to talk to a guy who was headed to Columbus, Ohio. We got to talking and I asked him if he was married. He said yes, happily. I told him my girlfriend was being stalked by her ex and he'd put a tracker on her car to follow her. He wanted to hurt her. This guy got upset and said that's not right.

"We worked out an arrangement. His company has trucks going in all directions. He said to give him the tracker and he'd make sure that when he got to Columbus, he'd have a fellow trucker take it south to maybe Georgia or Florida and send word to have it go west to Texas or Arizona but never toward northern California.

"I gave the guy a hundred bucks for his help. He put the tracker in an official company envelope and sealed it up. Your tracker will be sent back and forth all over the country."

"This is so good. Thank you."

A half hour later Matt found an empty space in front of the rental car office at the Coeur d'Alene airport and parked.

"I'll turn in the car, and we can walk over to where my plane is located. It should be fueled and ready to go. Grab your bag and I'll be right back."

Matt punched the button to open the hatch and got out. He and Tawnya unloaded the car and she stood next to their backpacks while he entered the office.

Ten minutes later they walked to the flight line. It was a cool night but not uncomfortable with clear skies. Would be a good night to fly.

"How long have you been a pilot?" Tawnya shifted her backpack to avoid her incision.

"In 2008 my dad took me for my first flight that I piloted on my own. Before that I had been his co-pilot several times. So, I guess fifteen years or so."

"What kind of plane?"

"Single engine prop until I joined the marines and became a jet pilot. F-16s in Afghanistan. Two tours."

"In war?"

"Well, it wasn't called a war officially but yes we inflicted damage."

"I think I feel better about flying with you now." She hurried to keep up.

"That's it over there. The white one. Stow your bag behind the seat and I'll get us a flight plan and check in. Probably be best if you stay with the plane."

"Okay."

Twenty minutes later they donned headsets and strapped themselves in. Matt flicked switches and lights came on inside. Tawnya watched intently as he readied the plane for takeoff.

"Have you ever flown in a small plane before?"

"Yes, a couple of times. I did not like it." She adjusted her seatbelt and leaned back in her seat.

"Did you throw up?"

"No. I did not." She slapped his arm.

Matt flinched and contacted flight control. Within minutes they cleared him to taxi to the runway approach. When he reached Runway 2, he received the all clear for takeoff and revved the engine.

Liftoff was smooth. Matt checked his heading and turned into his route coordinates. He glanced at Tawnya. She had her nose pressed to the side window taking in the lights of the city as they winged their way west.

"How long will our flight be?"

"About fourteen hours. We'll make a stop probably in Portland for some rest and refueling. Maybe do some sightseeing there. How about that?"

"I would like this. I have never been sightseeing. What do we do?"

"We look at something we find interesting, and we investigate it. We will know what it is when we see it. The fun is not knowing before."

Chapter 12

New York LaGuardia Airport
Private cargo depot

"Pietor, my old friend. How are you?" Dmitri Oborin waved the man up into the cargo hold of a Polish airliner. He and two others had flown from Warsaw to New York to pick Pietor up and continue to Spokane.

"I am well. I had not realized we were old friends." Pietor took the offered hand to help climb aboard.

"We were comrades in our training. I thought we bonded quite well."

"There was no bonding during training. Only the will to survive and finish above ground. There were times when I was not sure I would make it. I have been thankful that I went through it. My life has been saved from those lessons many times."

"And we now work together so we must be friends, no?" Dmitri signaled the pilot and a few seconds later the hatch closed, and the men took uncomfortable seats attached to the side of the plane.

The engines revved up and Dmitri handed Pietor a set of headphones. Even then they had to almost yell to be heard.

"I was told you would have supplies for me."

"Those four bags hold everything we need. You get one of them." Dmitri pointed to four duffels strapped together with other cargo.

"Good. I would like to take a look at the gear."

"Be my guest. These other two men are Symon Koval and Sasha Lebedev. They are Ukrainian but do not hold that against them. They are fighters, well qualified."

Pietor nodded at the two men who returned the nod. He got up and unlatched the duffels. He opened one and rummaged inside. He sighed. Two SR-2 Udav pistols, an eight-inch tactical knife, five magazines, a first aid kit, a box of twelve ready-to-eat meals, articles of camouflaged clothing, night vision goggles, and an SVT-40 battle rifle with three ten round magazines.

He zipped it back up and reattached it to the others and returned to his seat.

The trip west was noisy, uncomfortable, and bereft of conversation. They had been fully briefed on their mission. Bring her back whether dead or drugged. Preferably alive.

Sasha directed his team to a car rental counter upon arrival in Spokane. They then found a motel and secured two rooms next to each other. The two Ukrainians in 114 and Pietor and Sasha in 112. They unloaded their gear and gathered in Dmitri's room.

"Here we are in the life of luxury. Are we enjoying ourselves?" Sasha waved his hands at the typical twin bed motel room.

"This is nicer than some of the homes I have lived in." Symon remarked.

"Enough. We are not here for a vacation. We have work to do." Sasha pulled his phone out of his pocket. He swiped to the tracking screen.

"No. What is happening? Tawnya is moving. She is no longer here. The tracker shows her on a highway somewhere in Montana driving east. I need to call

Gregor to determine what he wants us to do and let him know we have arrived." He dialed Gregor's number.

"Sasha, where are you?" Gregor's voice rasped loudly. He was on speaker.

"Spokane. We have rented rooms and a car. Tawnya has…"

"I can see that. She is heading east. Do you know anything?"

"No. We just got in our rooms five minutes ago. Have not had time to unpack even. What do we do?"

"Nothing we can do till she stops, and we locate her. Sit tight and don't draw attention to yourselves. Call me when she stops." Gregor hung up.

His second glass of vodka did not satisfy Gregor as it usually did. He stared out his window at the guard circling his property. Two huge dogs practically pulled the man along, eager to find and tear into anything that did not belong.

He was proud of his guard dogs. Four Caucasian Ovcharka males, known as shepherd or mountain Caucasians, they were powerful animals most often used in Russian prisons. Weighing over one hundred pounds each they could rip a man to shreds in less than a minute. Who would not feel safe with them patrolling his dacha?

What made him feel unsafe was not having Tawnya in his control. Thankfully few people knew his secret, but none of them would hesitate to punish him for losing her. He worried about how long he could keep her disappearance quiet. His life literally depended upon keeping it to himself.

He sipped his drink and sat down. Tawnya's unopened file occupied the left corner of the six-foot-wide Russian beechwood desk. The top was empty except for her file. He pulled the thick folder toward him and flicked open the cover.

The blonde woman glaring back at him from an eight by ten glossy revealed an eternal smirk which highlighted her dimples. Her look was do-not-mess with me. The weapon pointed at the photographer, a Russian long range Dragunov SVD accurate up to twelve hundred meters, rested comfortably in her hands, even though it weighed more than a comparable US M-4. Her scores exceeded all other competitors.

Why had he sent her to America? Even though her assignment was basically designated as another assassination target, she had been all over Europe and Africa. He mentally slapped himself for not anticipating she might succumb to the lure of being on her own. In Europe he had much more latitude to keep her in check. Many more assets to attach her to.

The day she came to him and asked when she would be able to live her own life, marked the beginning. Many assassins burned out after four or five years. She now had nine years in service. The indicators readily making their way to the surface. He thought he had no other choice but to send her. Now he regretted not attempting to find another solution.

Gregor thought of her as a dependent, not quite as a daughter. When she first arrived, his intent was to groom her as almost a concubine. However, once her abilities materialized there was no hiding her. She had innate spy characteristics everyone acknowledged, and her destiny became inevitable.

He finished his drink and lolled in his chair. His predicament necessitated a strategy for insuring his survival. He just was not certain what that strategy entailed.

Where are you, my pet? He pressed his hand on her cheek in the photo. *What is your goal? Let me bring you back without harming you. But do not underestimate me. In the end my life is more precious than yours. Do not make me choose.*

Chapter 13

After a layover and refueling in Eugene Oregon, the trip to San Jose was uneventful, landing smoothly at Mineta International Airport. They taxied to Matt's hanger and pulled inside the open door. He arranged for servicing and inspection with the attendant who had prepared the hanger for his arrival, and they unloaded their backpacks.

"How was the trip?" Matt picked up Tawnya's pack.

"I can take the pack. I enjoyed very much the trip and the sightseeing." She held out her hand.

"I got the pack we're only going a few feet." He pointed to a blue F-150.

"Is yours?"

"Yup. My ride is more comfortable than it looks."

He stretched and thought he heard a bone crack. Ten hours of flying can put a crimp in anyone's back. He walked up to the truck and placed the packs in the bed. They climbed in and he pushed the start button.

"Buckle up, next stop home."

"I have no home. I will have one someday. In the meantime, I will stay at your home for a short time. Thank you for helping me."

The late afternoon June sun beat down and Matt was thankful for the rush of cool air inside. Highway I-880 was as usual crowded.

"I enjoyed seeing the ocean on our flight. I have

always wanted to see the Pacific."

"We won't be far from the ocean. We can visit tomorrow if you like." Matt grinned.

"Oh yes, I would like. It is so beautiful. Already I want to live here."

"I have to tell you, it's not cheap to live in California. We need to find you a good paying job. But first we chill and relax."

"What is chill? I hear people say that a lot."

"A slang for take it easy. "

"Why not just say relax? I do not always understand American slang words."

"Hey, you do well. Your English is very good with just a slight accent."

"Also, I will find a job myself. You have done enough for me. My job will be sufficient to pay you back."

"Now wait right there. No talk of paying back. I'm helping because it's the right thing to do. This is something to learn about Americans. Most of us are willing to give you a hand. We pride ourselves in being generous."

"Okay, when I become an American, I will also be generous."

Matt hoped she would do just that. Forty minutes after landing they turned onto a hard dirt road and approached a fence that seemed to go on forever. A gate entrance opened squeakily when Matt entered a code on a pad attached to the gatepost. He pulled in and the gate swung shut behind them.

The road led up a hill and as they reached the top Tawnya gasped.

"I love mountains. Those buildings down there are

yours?"

"They are. My dad bought this place after he sold his business. He made enough to buy it outright, so I'm blessed to have no mortgage. He named the place, Rancho Elaine, my mom's name. It's pretty much self-sustaining. We offer a hiking and hunting service, and we sell the cattle to local butchers.

"And a couple times a year in September, we offer a dude ranch experience." She had a questioning look. "A dude ranch is where city folks come and pay to live a week or two on a ranch."

"People pay for this?"

"Yes, and we make them work too."

"Very strange." Tawnya shook her head.

They continued down the road. A mile and a half later a huge house fashioned from a combination of wood and stone commanded attention. It seemed to burst from the hill behind it. Almost part of the mountains circling the valley. Three stories of Spanish architecture rose out of the scrub brush encrusted hard ground. Two arches surrounded double wooden entry doors. The first floor featured two oversized bay windows and wrought iron balconies garnished the upper floors.

"Is not a house. Is a palace." Tawnya remarked.

"Dad wanted plenty of space. He fell in love with this place the minute he drove out here."

"Ya, what is not to love?"

Matt parked on the rock drive in front of the nine steps up to the porch. A man rushed out of one of the front doors and jumped down the steps.

"Hey, bro, great to see ya." As Matt got out the man enveloped him in a bear hug. Then he stepped back as Tawnya hopped down out of the passenger seat.

"Whoa. You didn't tell me you were bringin' a movie star with ya." He took off his cowboy hat and waved it in a low bow, his two-foot-long braid of auburn hair swinging in front of him. "Rich Garnett, at your service ma'am."

"Rich, good to see you, too. This is Tawnya. She'll be staying here for a few days."

"It's an honor, Tawnya. Anything I can do to make your stay more pleasurable; you just holler."

Tawnya swirled to take in the view.

Rich gave Matt a wink. "Nice work, my man."

"Let's get Tawnya settled in her room and we can sit down and talk."

"What room do you want for her?" Rich began hefting backpacks out of the truck. He made it look easy. His solid six-foot-four-inch frame easily carried his two hundred fifteen pounds.

"The West bedroom will be fine." He lifted his pack off Rich's shoulder. "I'll put my stuff in my room and let's meet in the library in half an hour. That'll give you a chance to check out your room, Tawnya."

"If I can find this library. I am destined to be lost multiple times in such a large home."

"Don't worry, little lady. I'll take you on a tour. Not hard to find your way. Follow me." Rich took the stairs two at a time and opened one of the double doors for her. He gave Matt another wink.

Matt shook his head and joined them at the door.

Tawnya followed the cowboy inside. He was trying hard to impress her. He has a long way to go, she thought. Then she stopped and her mouth dropped open. The lobby she had entered would have been adequate for a five-star hotel. The ceiling went to the top of the house.

A sunken living room featured a big square in the lobby. The sofas and chairs covered with western blankets could easily seat twenty-five people. On either side of the living area matching stone staircases led to the second and third floors.

The far end of the lobby held the dining area and kitchen. Eight chairs faced each other across a long table with another chair at each end. On the sides under the staircases the doors to two rooms were visible. She estimated the width of the inside room to be at least eighty feet and the ceiling forty feet.

The only house she had been in of this size was Gregor's dacha outside Saint Petersburg. That house was dark and eerie, cold and damp. The sun's rays flooded this one and even without lights it was brightly lit and smelled wonderful, a mixture of pine and something baking. Her stomach growled.

"This way ma'am. Your room awaits." Rich clomped up the stairs to the left and Tawnya, her head on a constant swivel, followed.

"This room is a guest room and the next one is a bathroom, then another guest room, and we get to yours." Rich pointed with his left hand to the rooms. "Across the hall are other guest rooms. Here is yours." He opened a door and they entered.

"Oh my, this is mine?"

A king size bed sat in the middle covered with four decorator pillows, and two six-drawer dressers flanked it. A sofa and a leather easy chair sat to one side and an antique roll top desk rested across the room.

Rich placed her backpack on an old-fashioned trunk at the end of the bed. He pointed to a door to the left of the bed.

"That's your bathroom. Should be plenty of towels and whatnot. If you need anything Sandra will be here tomorrow. She does the cleaning and cooking. Just ask. I'll let you freshen up. You're welcome to take a shower. Anything else I can do for you?"

"Um, the library?"

"Oh gosh. Silly me I forgot. As you come in the house downstairs it's the second door on the right. The door will be open. If ya get lost, holler out. We'll hear ya." He grinned.

"Thank you, Rich. I appreciate your help."

He did a half bow and left.

She went to take a peek at the bathroom. Suddenly a shower was just what she needed. Ten minutes later she did something she had not remembered doing in well, forever. She sat on the bed and laughed.

It came when she unpacked her backpack, placed her meager items in two of the dresser drawers and asked out loud, "What do I put in the other ten drawers?" Laughter never came spontaneously. She could not remember many times being happy.

Once when she had first held her baby boy. Perhaps the only time in her life she was truly happy. Motherhood a foreign concept for her which came unexpected and unwelcomed at first. But when that fat dimpled face grinned up at her, her heart almost exploded. A pathway to suppressed emotions opened wide. She had help from a gypsy woman who worked on the training base, teaching Tawnya how to care and nurture Sergei.

Then as usual life threw her into an abyss. Sergei developed pneumonia and died just short of his first birthday celebration. As if that were not enough her husband was killed in Syria two months later, when a cloud of serin gas caught a wrong gust of wind and blew back into nine Spetsnaz soldiers.

From then on, her life became robotic. She did not know how to mourn so she completed assignments seemingly with no regard for her safety. No, for Tawnya any semblance of the so-called good life ceased to materialize. You get up in the morning, complete your duties and if you don't die during the day you go to bed and repeat the next day.

Maybe when hiking in the mountains on rare occasions when spare time was allowed, she was happy. But happy enough to laugh? Comfortable enough? No. One thing she knew. She could get used to the happy feeling. But always there lurked the next catastrophic event she seemed doomed to endure.

Twenty minutes later, showered and refreshed, she left to try to find the library.

"Okay give me the story." Rich raised the beer to his lips and gulped.

"She was in trouble, and I helped her out. She has no place else to go. Some people are after her." They sat in leather chairs that redefined easy. Floor to ceiling bookcases easily containing five to six hundred books stood against each wall. An eight-foot round glass top table between them held their drinks. Iced tea for Matt.

"Who?" Rich leaned closer. "The mob, cartels, politicians. We need to call ghostbusters?"

"They were professionals. Not street punks or creeps. Well trained and not afraid to shoot first and never ask questions. Beyond that I don't know. Still getting pieces of her story."

"So anything else goin' on here?" Rich raised his eyebrows.

"No. Nothing. I swear. She's definitely Russian, Ukrainian, Eastern European. She says she grew up in Vermont. I doubt it. Worked in New York and was attacked there. Then when she got to Idaho, they found her and went after her again." Matt told Rich the story of his shortened stay there and the tracking device he had dug out of her and sent on its travels.

"What a great plan to send it across America. You think that will be the end of it?"

"You know what our training taught us. Never say never."

"Want to beef up security? I can call some guys."

"Not yet. Let's see what we can learn about these people from her first. She's going to have to come clean about who they are."

"Hello, Matt, Rich? Are you in there?"

"Here, Tawnya."

She came around the corner and stood beside Matt's chair. Her hair was wet from a shower, and she had changed to a pair of jeans and light blue blouse.

"Would you like something to drink? We have beer, soda, iced tea."

"I am partial to vodka if you have it." She sat in one of the chairs.

"Don't have any, but I'll put it on the grocery list. Do you have a brand preference?"

"No, you probably cannot get true Russian so anything, but definitely not a flavored vodka."

"Hey, Siri add vodka to the grocery list. How about some iced tea?" Siri let Rich know it was added.

"Fine, thank you."

Rich left to get Tawnya a drink.

"Did you get settled in?" Matt asked.

"I believe was the best shower I have ever had. I am refreshed."

Rich handed Tawnya her tea.

"What is plan for tomorrow?" Tawnya sipped her drink. "Um tea is good."

"Maybe we can visit the Pacific like you wanted."

"I would like this."

"However, we need to talk. You've told me a little about yourself, but you are holding back information we need to know. I think you know enough about me to realize I'm trying to help. I have no ulterior motive."

Tawnya stared at Matt but said nothing.

"Those men we escaped from in Idaho were professionals. I'm guessing they were Spetsnaz or at least KGB operatives. You obviously also had special training. So, your story about growing up in Vermont is not believable."

Still, she remained silent.

"Do you work for the Russian government? I think you are an operative yourself." Matt stared back at her.

"I do not work for the government. I swear that is true. But I can't tell you my background. I was trained by the KGB. I admit it. But I don't work for them. I quit. And I am serious about wanting to be an American. I am tired of my life and just want to be on my own."

"It's a fact that these people are out to either capture you or cause you harm. So, you are former KGB?"

"Yes, former. I was sent to New York on an assignment, and I finally refused to comply. I quit reporting to them, and I left to escape."

"What was the assignment?" Matt sat back.

"I cannot answer that. I now fight for my life. You must believe me."

"I do, but I don't want my home and my friends here to get hurt. I fear an attack might be coming. What are the chances whoever is after you would give up?"

"Humph. He would never give up. This is why I want to hide and go away from here. I do not wish you harm. You are good person and I appreciate your assistance. Just let me go. If they catch me, I will not tell them about you or this place. Please."

"Ma'am, speaking for myself, I will do everything I can to protect you while you're here. From what Matt told me of your attacks and the tracking device, you need some time to recuperate, and this seems as good a place as any. Matt, I hope I'm not speakin' out of turn."

"No, you're not. I was about to say the same thing."

"Thank you both."

"Something we talked about before is trust, Tawnya. You can trust us to do as we say. And I hope you will feel more comfortable with us to maybe tell us more of your story. It might help you come to grips with your situation and it might give us more information to strengthen our protection for you."

"I will think on this. I have much to think about. Much planning to do."

"I've had a chance to do some thinking also. One thing is, you are not a US citizen. Identification is going to be a serious problem at some point. As long as you're here your identity is not a matter of concern. Away from the ranch it will be.

"Second we need to beef up security and make this ranch a bit more lethal."

"We can do that. Oh yes." Rich rubbed his hands together and his grin was ear to ear.

"This I can help with. Do you have weapons?"

"Do we have weapons? Without a doubt. Can we show her our special corner, please?" Rich squirmed as he pleaded with Matt.

"Tomorrow, first we need to eat something and get a good night's rest. I'm beat." Matt finished his tea.

"I am hungry." Tawnya stood, picked up the empty glasses and headed to the kitchen. "I can do cooking."

"I think that might be a problem. Sandy does the cooking here and she allows very few to use her kitchen. She fixed up a bunch of sandwiches and fruit before she left tonight. Tomorrow, you'll meet her. Don't be put off by her manner. Down deep she's a sweetheart. Ya just have ta look hard for it sometimes." Rich shrugged and followed them.

Chapter 14

"She is in Minneapolis. Looks like she stopped for the night. I guess she rented a car for the trip to wherever. We will watch tomorrow to see what she does." Sasha munched on some peanut butter crackers.

"I had to release the other cargo plane because of paperwork. My private jet will be there tomorrow, and you can use it to fly to her destination." Gregor's voice echoed on his phone.

"How can a Russian plane travel anywhere in America? They are very strict."

"This is why you are the employee and not the employer. I have a company based in Paris to ferry people, materials, anything to just about anywhere in the world. A legitimate business, *Vin Exprimer*, delivering wine to wealthy people. Not just any wine but rare and expensive wine. They pay the high price, and on that plane, I include my shipments. They pay my shipping fees and also maintenance and landing fees." Gregor loved showing off his business acumen to underlings.

"We just call the pilot when we determine where we should go?"

"Precisely. Give him time to set up a valid flight plan. He will be ready when you get there." Gregor recited the phone number of his pilot and hung up.

Now that he had everything in place all he had to do was wait, and pour money into this delay for rooms, food, booze, and probably other things he would rather not know about.

The next several days tested and tried Gregor's patience. Tawnya traveled from Minneapolis to Columbus, OH and stayed one night. On to Atlanta, GA where she stayed one day and continued to Gainesville, FL, the next day to Mobile, AL. Gregor yelled into his phone each time he contacted Sasha. His voice was wearing down and he did not enjoy his geography lesson about America.

Next stop was Houston, then Amarillo, TX. On day eleven of his frustration Tawnya finally stopped in Albuquerque, NM. None of Gregor's men or Gregor himself were able to pronounce the name. They referred to it as Al.

On day twelve four men, two of them with nasty hangovers, flew to Albuquerque to deliver wine. And capture Tawnya. Gregor had to order more vodka to refill his private stock. It had never been so perplexing. He was apoplectic by this time screaming at his uncaring phone.

"Are you sure? She's in that truck?" Sasha asked.

"I just read what the tracker says. Now it says she's in that truck. Where is the driver?" Dimitri asked.

"Still in the house. He brought a couple of bags of food about an hour ago and went inside." Symon whispered. He strolled by the house, Dimitri and the two others sat in their rental a block away on a side street. The semi parked beside a small ranch home at the end of the road had been there for two days.

"Wait the door is opening. A man is coming out. The driver. He's going to smoke. He is sitting on the steps and puffing away." Symon turned and headed back to the car.

"Tracker still shows her in the truck. Maybe she is hiding and waiting for the truck to go somewhere else. Wait there Symon. We are coming."

Dimitri put the car in drive and weaved around the car parked in front of him. They picked up Symon and stopped in front of the smoking man.

"Wait in car for my signal. Then we clear the inside and check out the truck."

Dmitri jumped out and walked toward the man. He checked to make sure no one else was around.

"Hello, could you help with directions? I am lost."

The man stood and flicked ashes into the yard. He was chunky, a nice American word for fat, bald, wearing thick glasses, and had a full beard.

"Sure but I ain't from here. I'll try though."

Dmitri held out his hand to shake. "Thanks, Mr…?"

"Sanderson, I…"

Dmitri grabbed the outstretched hand and yanked Sanderson to the ground forcing his arm up behind him. He signaled to the car and the three hurried up the steps and into the house.

"Ow. What's this all about? That hurts."

"Relax Mr. Sanderson. We need to ask a question and then we'll be gone. Where's the girl?"

"Myra? She's in the house."

Dmitri glanced at the house where Symon carried a large woman, also a nice American word for fat, under one arm. She wriggled but could not escape his grasp.

"Lemme go ya big ape. Wait till I get upright." She punched Symon in the stomach three times, and he dropped her on the porch.

She wobbled to her feet and attempted another punch. Symon hopped back and as she leaned in to throw another, Symon jabbed his fist into her jaw. She fell face down onto the wood flooring.

"What's going on? Don't hurt her. Tell me what you want." Sanderson struggled to breathe with Dimitri's foot across his neck.

"I'm going to let you up. We will sit on the step. You can smoke. We will talk. Yes?"

"Right. Whatever you say."

They let Sanderson get up and sit on the steps. He adjusted his glasses.

"I'm going to reach for my cigarettes, okay?"

Dimitri nodded.

While he lit up, he glanced at Myra and shook his head.

"I'm all ears fellas. Ask away."

"What is in the truck?"

"Nothin' right now. I'm waitin' for a pick up. Probably be one tomorrow or the next day."

"We wish to look inside."

"Sure, no problem. This way boys." He lifted himself off the stairs and walked to the rig. At the back he unlocked the door and stepped back. "Help yerself."

As he said it was empty. They even checked for a hiding place for contraband. Nothing.

"Let us see the cab." Dimitri pointed to the driver door.

Sanderson unlocked and opened the door. Dimitri climbed in and searched. He found an envelope in the dash compartment.

"What is this?" He held up the envelope.

"Oh, are you the ex?"

"Ex?"

Sanderson relayed the story they had been given and

Dimitri felt like slapping himself. Of course, the woman had sent them chasing the wild goose.

They hauled Myra into the living room and suggested Sanderson should get her some ice. They sat in the living room and discussed in Russian what to do next while Sanderson tried to revive his girlfriend. Dimitri assigned Symon to take the two into the back bedroom and find out if they knew where Tawnya was and where she was last spotted.

An hour later Gregor's phone chirped.

"You have her, yes?"

"We have the chip but unfortunately not her."

"Explain, please." Gregor ground his teeth so hard he thought one of his fillings cracked.

"Tawnya being a smart woman, had the tracker taken out and placed in an envelope which was transported all over the country. We found the last trucker in Al and heard the story."

"Did you find where she is now?"

"No. We interrogated the couple who live here, and they know nothing. Just couriers."

"And?"

"They will talk to no one. Ever again. Seems to have been a terrible domestic argument. The Mrs. stabbed the man and he shot her. We were sure to use the man's pistol. Neither survived. Are resting in their dining room."

Dmitri held the phone away from his ear. The three-minute tirade came through loud and clear.

"Back to the beginning again. We need you to go back to Idaho and find a lead. Someone knows something. Dig until you find her." He slammed the phone on the desk three times before it exploded.

Thirteen days chasing an envelope.

The luxuries on Gregor's plane had never even been imagined by the any of the four men. It took only an hour to clear out his snack bar and stash of booze. Stuffed full of treats and properly buzzed they spread out and dropped into a symphony of snores. The two-thousand-mile trip back to Spokane took four hours and when they arrived, they were well rested, although with throbbing headaches.

Chapter 15

The waves smashing against the rocks surrounding the small cove sent a sea mist of salt filled spray blanketing Matt and Tawnya every minute or so. The sun's rays bursting through the cloudless sky warmed the drops quickly. The temperature hovering around seventy-five left them comfortable in swimwear.

"It is so beautiful. The ocean seems to be breathing, so alive. Thank you for bringing me here." She lifted her arms and turned in a circle trying to absorb every detail. The ocean smell of fish and kelp filled her nostrils as she tasted the salty droplets.

They had stopped at a local store to fill out her wardrobe including a multicolored two-piece swimsuit. She had wanted only a couple of blouses and jeans, but Matt had piled enough to fill three huge shopping bags. Tawnya wanted to ask how he could afford the expenses she was costing him. All he would say when she even a mentioned it, he was able to afford whatever she needed.

She edged out to the water.

"It's gonna be cold. Too cold to swim." Matt held up his hands.

"You forget I am from Russia."

Before Matt could say or do anything she rushed into the surf and dove into the ocean. The water took her breath for a few seconds, then felt invigorating, an adrenalin rush. She reverted to her swimming competitions and continued under water in a long kick till she surfaced and looked back.

The cove was calm compared to the waters beyond the breakers encircling the cove. No strong currents and undertows, just smooth clear water. She noticed Matt waving his arms and shouting. For sure he was concerned about her, so she quickly swam to the shore. Her strokes even and strong, she made it back easily and pulled herself up.

Matt broke into the water and wrapped his arms around her prying her out to usher her to the beach.

"What are you doing? Hypothermia is nothing to play around with, Tawnya. Let's build a fire. Come over here." He tugged her to a spot far enough away from the water and began gathering anything close that would burn.

"I am fine. Do not worry. I am good swimmer." She used her blouse from their pile of clothes to dry off.

Matt said nothing but continued building his firepit. When the fire erupted and he had piled more deadwood onto it he grabbed her hand and guided her over.

"Matt, I am not a little girl to be corrected and coddled. Please, I am good."

"Yeah, shivering indicates your complete comfort." He frowned.

"When I was sixteen, I trained to be Olympic swimmer. The facility I swam in was kept at cold temperature to make sure we could endure extreme conditions. Then at KGB facility their pool was even colder. I grew up dealing with the cold."

"I'm sorry, I just got concerned when you disappeared for like a full minute. I also underwent impossible swimming conditions. I hated it."

"For your solace, the fire feels good. Thank you." She wrapped her arms around herself.

"How is your wound? Healing, okay?"

She lifted her arm and patted the fresh bandage. "Is good. I can move with little pain. The swim felt good. I have not been swimming for some time. I need to begin exercising again. Running and something to strengthen my muscles."

"We have an exercise room on the ranch. When we get back, I'll show it to you. Use it whenever you wish."

"Do you know judo or jujitsu?" She raised her eyebrows.

"Maybe a little. Wanna work out together?" Matt grinned.

"I would like this. I know you stopped the man at the restaurant, and he was trained. We will see what you can do."

"Just don't hurt me." He laughed.

"What is it you Americans say, no pain, no gain? Pain is expected in confrontations, is it not?"

"Frankly, I've never been a fan of getting hurt. Go easy on me, please." He got up and doused the fire with sand. They dressed, climbed the incline to the car and returned to the ranch.

Rich greeted them as they pulled in front of the ranch house. Matt parked behind a high-end black SUV.

"So how was it, Tawnya?" He opened the passenger door and waited for her to step down.

"Words do not describe how beautiful. I even took a swim." She shook her wet head.

"I bet that woke ya up. Had to be a mite chilly."

"Was moderately cold." She grinned.

"Sandy has arrived. Let's go meet her." Matt hoisted

two shopping bags out of the back.

Rich took the last bag, and they climbed the steps.

Inside the smells stopped Tawnya.

"What do I smell? Something wonderful."

"That's my homemade spaghetti, my dear. And garlic toast." A throaty voice yelled from the back. "Be right there."

Matt handed Rich his bags and motioned for him to take them to Tawnya's room. He nodded and took the three bags up the steps.

"You must be Tawnya. I've been hearin' about you so much I feel like I know ya. I'm Sandy." A short woman rushed out of the kitchen and grabbed Tawnya's hand and gave it a quick shake. A red and white apron folded around an ample stomach was emblazoned with the saying, "Don't mess with the chef. You'll get spatulated." Her hair was uncombed gray and speckled with green tints. Gray eyes sparkled behind granny glasses.

"So glad to meet you, Sandy. The smells from the kitchen are making my legs melt."

"Oh, gosh, I got to stir. Lunch'll be ready in about ten minutes. Be right back. Set yourself at the dining room table. Ya want some iced tea?" She waved a large spoon as she turned, her wrinkled face frowning.

Matt waved her to the kitchen. "I'll get it, you go stir."

She hurried off.

"I will go get my hair dry and change clothes. Iced tea would be nice." She turned and went upstairs.

Matt opened the refrigerator and fixed tea for her and one for himself.

"Is she a Commie, Matt?" Sandy whispered over her

shoulder.

"We've never discussed it in those terms. She's in trouble and needs some help."

"Don't want no Commie runnin' around here." She frantically stirred the sauce.

"I'll let you evaluate her yourself. Just don't come right out and ask her. Okay?"

Matt couldn't decipher what Sandy muttered but it was sure to be addressed later. He went to place the teas on the table.

Rich came down and stopped at the kitchen door. "Can I get a beer, Sandy?"

"Proper request is, may I have a beer." She opened the fridge and threw him a bottle.

"Yes, ma'am." He caught the beer and twisted it open. "Why do I always feel like I'm in the first grade again around here?" he said softly.

"I heard that. Can't help my teacher background. Just pops up once in a while." The oversized spoon resumed clanking against the side of the pan.

"Once in a while?"

"I heard that, too." Clank, clank.

Ten minutes later they all sat at the huge dining room table. Perched on the top were spaghetti, salad, garlic bread and a pitcher of iced tea. Tawnya sat on the side next to Matt, Sandy sat opposite them, and Rich sat at the head. All bowed their heads except Tawnya who was reaching for the bread to pass around.

"My dear around here at meals we thank God for his bounty." Sandy glared at Tawnya.

"Please forgive me. I am not familiar with your customs or your god." She set the bread down and bowed her head. Her eyes gazed up at the group.

Sandy said the prayer and they began passing food back and forth.

"I appreciate that you don't know about our customs, and that's okay. Do you believe in God?" Sandy spooned out a generous helping of spaghetti.

"I have heard of God, but he has not made himself present to me. My life has been filled with protecting myself, relying on myself for everything. It's all I know. This very good. Thank you." She slurped a wayward spaghetti strand through her lips.

Rich's eyes pivoted from Sandy to Tawnya, and then Matt.

"Sandy, Tawnya wants to become an American. She would like to get away from her former job and the life she had before." Matt twirled a bite of noodles with his fork.

Sandy nodded then swallowed. "I have a question then. Are you a communist?"

Rich gagged and took a quick drink. Matt rolled his eyes. Tawnya laughed.

"I am not a communist. I guess I do not know what I am yet. I am anxious to learn more about America." She waved her fork at Sandy. "I will tell you this. In my life men, all men, have never been kind to me, until I arrived here. In every country I have been, and there are many, men only wanted one thing from me.

"American men have never been anything but helpful and kind. I admire and am honored by that. This is why I want to be an American. I feel respected and this feeling I have never experienced in my life." She chewed off a hunk of garlic bread.

"In my book that's all I needed to hear. I'd love to talk to you about what America means to me. How about it?"

"This I would very much like, Mrs. Sandy." She nodded.

It seemed the whole table breathed a sigh of relief and the meal resumed with gusto.

"And it's just Sandy. Lose the Mrs. part. Okay?"

"Yes, Sandy."

Chapter 16

Two hours later, Matt and Tawnya reined in their horses returning from a tour of the ranch. A visit to California vistas Tawnya had only found in searches online heightened her anticipation of the many hikes into the surrounding mountains Matt had promised.

The spring-fed reservoir where they had stopped, rated a designation of a breathtaking sight in Tawnya's mind. They tied their horses to a stout bush, and she watched Matt unload gear from his saddlebags. He pulled out a shovel and showed it to Tawnya.

"I will get us some bait. Dig for worms."

Ten minutes later Matt placed eight fat wiggly earthworms on a pile of leaves.

"Have you ever been fishing, Tawnya?" Matt sat rods and reels and a tackle box at the edge of the small lake.

"No. I buy my fish at the market." She grinned. She had not made a joke many times before.

"This is like a hobby or something people do on vacations. We throw a baited line into the pond and try to get a fish to bite. Then we haul it in and cook it for dinner." He snapped two rods together and began baiting the hooks. He decided not to try teaching fly fishing. They would just shore cast.

"My way is more efficient, I think."

"I agree but just the thrill of catching one is

contagious. Will you try?"

"Of course. I will be good at this."

"Takes patience." He lifted his forefinger.

"I have patience. In my work it is vital for success."
She narrowed her eyebrows.

"Spy work?" Matt wiggled his eyebrows.

"In Russia the word is *spionam*. Do you know the
word?"

Matt shook his head.

"It means spy. But we do not discuss this. Show me
how to fish."

Soon Tawnya had mastered the casting of her line.
They sat on two small boulders obviously placed for just
that reason.

Two minutes later Matt landed a good-sized bass.
He threaded it onto a line he tossed back in the water and
cast once more. Tawnya watched him as he sat waiting
for another bite.

"What are you doing with your finger?"

"I have it above the rod so that when a fish is
nibbling at the bait, I can feel it and set the hook. Try it."

She did as he said and waited. Soon she felt tugging
and pulled in the line. No fish appeared but the bait was
gone. Matt showed her how to attach another bait. She
cast again. Matt pulled in one more fish. He said nothing
and continued.

After fifteen minutes Matt had two more fish and
Tawnya had missed three times. She threw down the rod.

"Is boring. I do not like to fish."

"It takes practice, and you'll learn when to set the
hook." He reeled in his line.

"Is not for me. I will continue to visit the fish
market."

Matt worked with her and soon she had her first catch.

"I have one. What do I do?"

"Hold tight. Let the fish go where it wants but keep the line tight. That's it. Pull it gently toward you. Wind the reel at the same time."

"I do not want to lose this thing. How embarrassing this would be." She finally pulled the tired fish onto the pond's edge and after Matt told her where to grab it, she held it up.

"Is bigger than any of yours. See I am natural." She grinned.

"Success. You're the champ." Matt gave her a high five.

'You have more than me. I think you are champ."

"But you got the biggest one. That decides it."

She let Matt attach it to the others and stood back. She did a full turn to take in the view.

"I am in love with this place. You are so lucky to live here. Someday I hope to be so lucky. I wish to thank you again for helping me."

Matt broke down the fishing gear and repositioned it on his horse. Matt looked across the meadow at his ranch house.

"I wish the same for you Tawnya. Now let's get these beauties back to clean and have Sandy do her magic cooking."

"I am eager to taste my fish."

"I want to apologize for Sandy's bluntness at lunch. She's protective of me and the ranch. She only wants me to be happy."

"You may be surprised to learn I like Sandy. I value people who are straight forward and who let you know what they are thinking. Is rare trait. We will become friends I think."

"Good to hear. Sandy is like my mother. When I lost my parents, she stepped in."

"Is also why I like her. She is deep down good."

"Tomorrow we will go for a long hike. How is your wound doing?"

"Is good as new almost." She patted her side roughly. "All okay."

They mounted and headed back to the ranch.

At the stable a short man with wavy coal black hair and a heavy horseshoe mustache greeted them and held Tawnya's horse as she dismounted. Matt swung down and slapped Joe on the back.

"Tawnya, this is Joe Sanchez. She's my guest and has the run of the place, Joe." Matt winked.

"Glad to meet you, Miss Tawnya. I'll tend your horse for you." He patted the horse's neck.

"Thank you. I can do it." She grabbed the reins.

"'Cuse me, ma'am, but as a guest you are not required to do that. It's why I'm here. And if I don't do it, Matt will kick my butt. Please, he kicks hard." Joe grunted.

"Then I feel I am saving you from a dire fate. You may go." She handed him the lead.

Joe jerked Matt's as well and sauntered off. "He's a mean man, Lady. Just plain mean."

"Are you mean, Matt?" Tawnya smiled.

"Only when provoked. But you know that. Joe is a good man. Worked here for lemme see…about two years I think."

They walked back to the house.

"Have I met everyone who works here?"

"One other man who I would guess is out checking fences, Riley Walters. Never ending job that is. They are kind of interchangeable. Tending to the horses and stock. Others come and go with the seasons. When we have our dude ranch days, four more guys and one gal from around here take up residence. That'll be in September."

"Will be busy I am betting."

"Oh yes. Likes to kill me sometimes keeping things straight and easy for the paying customers."

"You have six horses?"

"Normally, but we add more with our hands who bring their own mounts and a couple more for the patrons. By the way, I'm impressed with your riding ability. You handled your horse like a pro."

"As a teenager one of the orphanages I lived in sat next to a riding stable, and we were able to learn how to ride. Many hours spent in the saddle. Was the only thing I found enjoyable. We had competitions with the offspring of the owners."

"I bet you won."

"Most of the time. When I needed a favor or help, I would let one of the girls win. They knew it but we got along with them that way."

"Diplomacy personified."

"Yes. Also, I befriended a gypsy woman and she let me ride her horse. A beautiful *Budyony*, named *Po Poisku*, meaning sweet tooth. He loved sugar cubes. I had to steal them because they were reserved for the coffee of the headmaster."

"These horses are mustang rescues or mix breeds. Fine cattle horses. A bit stubborn sometimes." He laughed.

"I think most horses are that way."

"Right. Let's go get some food."

"This is best fish meal I have ever experienced, Sandy. You must teach me to cook. Only thing I know is microwave. Stick in machine, set time and blast the food. Simple." Tawnya mimicked pushing a button.

"Basic cooking is not hard. Now if we're talkin' gourmet that's another whole discussion. I can show you the basics. And millions of cookbooks are available with directions."

"Well, I will have time to learn. I am how you say it…retired." Tawnya grinned.

"What was your job?" Sandy asked.

Suddenly quiet engulfed the table. Matt squirmed and Rich gulped. Matt had given Rich a brief censured version of Tawnya's background. Sandy had not been briefed yet. Tawnya glanced at Matt and seemed to be waiting for him to answer.

"Tawnya's a former employee of the Russian government. An analyst of foreign entities. She was sent here to work in a Wall Street firm to observe and learn the financial business." Matt took a breath hoping that would suffice. It didn't.

"You are a spy?" Sandy's eyes sparkled.

"I suppose that would be correct." She finished her dinner and nodded at Matt.

"So, what's that like? I never met a spy before. Kinda like James Bond? I love those movies." Sandy leaned toward Tawnya. "I gotta know more. Please."

"Is not the glamorous life of movies. Dirty, nasty, and sometimes, yes, dangerous. This is why I quit. Not for me anymore. I do not like to remember this work."

"Oh, I'm sorry. I didn't mean to cause you

discomfort. It fascinates me is all. I read a lot of espionage and thriller novels. It's unbelievable someone even remotely connected to that would be sitting here next to me. I got excited. Forgive me." She patted Tawnya's hand.

"Not to worry."

"Okay, while we're on the subject, something I need to say. You guys, Tawnya has had people try to capture her and take her back to Russia. They are professionals who do not care if an innocent bystander gets hurt. There's a possibility that they may find out where she is and try again."

"They're gonna hafta go through me first." Rich rose halfway out of his chair.

"We believe that we've thrown them off our trail, but the possibility still exists. Again, they're adept at locating people. We're going to beef up our defenses just in case."

"Count me in." Rich replied.

"Me too." Sandy clinched her fists.

"Sandy your job will be to make sure the safe room is stocked and if we say go, you head there no questions asked. We don't want to have to worry about your safety. Promise?"

"I can handle a gun. My dad and I hunted a lot. I'm a dead shot with a rifle or a pistol. He had no son, so I became a bit of a tomboy." She placed her hands on her hips. "Lemme at 'em."

"Not a chance. You will have a gun in the safe room. That's it. I'm serious. Do this for me please." Matt's frown let her know he would not change his mind.

"All right. I'd hate to miss out on the fun though."

"That's my goal, for you to miss out. Rich, I have

several cameras for us to install and a few traps to set. We need to do that tomorrow. I have a computer setup in the office to monitor them. Also, we need a signal in case we have a problem. For a text, for vocal, phone call. A word we recognize tells us danger is imminent. This word triggers us into action.

"Sandy to the safe room, and Rich, Tawnya and I will go to our assigned places. Wherever we are we head to our spot and gear up. From now on we will wear protection and have a rifle near us. The word we will use is Vodka in honor of our guest. Everyone got that?"

A chorus of affirmative responses followed.

Chapter 17

Early the next morning at the barn Matt helped Rich check the ATV.

"She's ready to go." Rich closed the hatch. "Where ya goin'?"

"Thought we'd head up the valley through the north pass and try to locate the deer we spotted last week."

"I wish you luck. I can taste those venison steaks right now. Got plenty of room in the big freezer. I'll even help butcher." He tapped Matt's shoulder.

"Well, old friend, you and Riley will get to do that all by yourselves. I have paperwork to finish, and I need to order more feed and supplies."

"Crap! I knew there was a catch there somewhere." He slapped Matt's shoulder.

Tawnya joined them. Her long blonde hair tied in a ponytail and pulled through the back of a San Francisco Giants baseball cap. Jeans, a beige colored western blouse and new hiking boots completed her outfit. She looked younger today. Matt had estimated her age as middle thirties or more.

"How are you guys today?"

"Great." Both shouted at the same time.

"Wow, you look like a native Californian. Nice. Ready for the hunt, ma'am?" Rich grinned.

"Thank you. I am anxious to take in more of this beautiful scenery. Are we ready?"

"Climb in. Put your seat belt on because it can get mighty bumpy out there." Rich waved his hand toward the passenger seat.

Once seated Matt and Tawnya sputtered out of the barn.

The noise of the engine made it tough for conversation, so they enjoyed the views. Beyond the barn about two hundred yards, they opened the fence gate and motored through tall grass. As they approached a small creek that crossed the field Matt pulled up and stopped.

"This is a small tributary of the Guadalupe River." Matt pointed up to the hills. "In front of us is the Diablo Mountain range. That pass up there we'll go through gets us to the next valley. And then we'll begin our hunt."

"This is all so beautiful." She glanced around. "You own all of this?"

"We haven't reached the end of our property yet."

"You are lucky man, Matt."

"I guess. The way I see it, I'm just a caretaker till the next lucky guy comes along. In the meantime, I agree, I'm fortunate to be living here."

They crossed the creek and made their way through the pass. He pulled the ATV off to the side and stopped.

"We'll walk from here." Dismounting, he opened the storage bin retrieving two backpacks. He handed one to her and pulled out a rifle for her as well.

Tawnya slipped into the pack's straps and checked the rifle. Matt noticed how smoothly she handled the weapon. Although she'd never seen the pack and the rifle before, she handled them with familiarity.

He pulled out a pair of binoculars and panned the valley. "Don't see anything yet." He allowed her to do the same.

She slowly turned in a one-hundred-eighty-degree arc, then handed the glasses back to Matt. "There is a large bird in the grass that way. Is that our target?" She motioned down the hill.

"No, we're after deer. That's a turkey and we can always find them."

"Are they good to eat?"

"Oh my, yes. Sandy can make them taste so good. I think we have some in the freezer. We'll try to have a turkey dinner sometime. We're after bigger game this morning though."

He started off to the right instead of going down the hill. "We'll try for a better angle this way. Need to stay out of the wind so the deer don't catch our scent."

They wandered through the hills for another fifty minutes. Matt stopped and held up his hand. They crouched behind a pile of boulders resting on a small ledge. He pointed down the hill.

"You see it?"

"Yes. Deer?" She focused her eyes on the deer. The sun rising over the hill behind them highlighted the animal.

"A beauty. You want the shot?"

"Let me take a look." She rested her rifle on a four-foot-tall boulder and took aim. She sighted and then stopped.

"What's the matter?" Matt whispered.

"I have never had trouble pulling the trigger in my assignments. But now I don't know. They were enemy. This deer is not enemy. Is a fine animal, free and at home. Does not feel right to me. I am sorry. I do not want to shoot."

Matt cleared his throat. "That's okay, Tawnya. I understand." He chuckled. "You may be getting yourself Americanized quicker than you think."

"I do not understand." She frowned.

"You had feelings for the deer. You felt sorry for it. This is learning about your heart."

"You are not mad?"

"No. Not at all. I think we will let this deer live another day."

They stood and the deer's head popped up. He'd seen the movement and, in a heartbeat, bounded off deeper into the valley.

"Let's go back. Maybe we'll have that turkey dinner sooner than I expected." He grinned.

The silent trip back took an hour. Tawnya seemed confused and yet not upset. He could not imagine the jumble of emotions she now confronted. Maybe, most of them anyway, emotions totally foreign until today.

"I don't know what to think. I thought I would have no trouble on the hunt. Then when I took aim and that animal stared at me with the biggest brown eyes I have ever seen, I could not shoot it." Tawnya shrugged her shoulders.

They sat at the dining room table after a huge breakfast. Sandy refilled coffee cups, Matt and Rich listening intently as Tawnya recapped her hunt.

"Well, I for one think that is the best thing that's happened since you've been here, my dear. I've never shot a deer either. And those eyes. I know exactly what you mean." Sandy sat the pot on a mat on the table and took her seat.

"I sure was lookin' forward to a venison steak."

Rich shook his head.

"I'm sorry, Mr. Rich."

"Now wait a minute. I think what you did was just fine. There's a lot a people who couldn't shoot a deer. No shame in that."

"I feel I let you down." Her eyebrows furrowed.

"No, ya didn't. I'm just talkin', and a bit too much some might say."

"I might." Matt tilted his head at Rich.

"Figured it'd be you."

"Tawnya, remember yesterday you said you were just learning about your emotions. Today you learned a bunch. You have a good heart. Showing sympathy, even for an animal, is a positive for anyone." Sandy patted Tawnya's hand.

"I think we're all thinking the same thing. We'll pass on any future deer hunts," Matt said.

"Yes. A deal. But I could go on a turkey hunt. I do not like those birds. They have ugly, beady eyes." She grinned.

During the next few days, Tawnya felt truly free. She hiked the hills, enjoyed watching a little TV, learned a bit about cooking, and worked out in the exercise room. She embarrassed Rich by beating him in push-ups and almost lifted as much weight as he did.

They developed a workout routine that would tire a Navy Seal. Matt joined when he could, but he was no match for either of them whatever the activity. It was good to reach peak performance. She felt she could tackle just about anything.

She didn't know if this was what it felt like to be happy, truly happy, but it rivaled the time in that Russian hospital when her newborn son had looked up at her for the first time with eyes open. Her whole body had shivered with joy.

There was a time when she wondered why she wanted to live. What was her purpose? Why not just check out? She had envisioned putting her gun to her head and pulling the trigger. No more sadness, no more responsibilities, no more submitting to every whim of some pathetic political authority. Just end it to gain peace.

Now though, she had hope for a chance at a life she could control. Determine her own path and not be subject to unreasonable demands or activities. That was something to live for.

Matt, Rich and Sandy had reinforced her belief in the good of America. She did not want to overstay her welcome. She would have to find a job to earn a living. Something in banking or brokerage management would get her started. She wanted to be totally on her own.

Still in the back of her mind the threat of Gregor and the KGB remained. She needed time to determine if she was out of the line of fire from them. She would stay here for a short bit of time and then begin her new life.

Chapter 18

Sandy stood at the sink drying the last of the breakfast dishes. The blue sky devoid of clouds allowed a great view of an eagle gliding through the upper winds. The giant wings wove a path for the bird around the corral to the north of the ranch house searching for its next meal.

She immediately thought of Tawnya's search for freedom. Hopefully she would find her own chance for independence. She sighed as Tawnya entered the kitchen and stood looking like she wanted to say something.

"We have some coffee left in the pot if you want some." Sandy pointed to the side counter.

"I thought maybe some tea. Not much of a coffee person."

"Of course. There are some tea bags in that cupboard, and I'll put on some water for you. Sit, we can talk." Sandy busied herself filling a pot at the sink.

"Where are Matt and Rich?" Tawnya asked.

"Went to pick up an order of supplies. Be back in an hour or so."

"After tea I might hike into the hills for a while. I hate to waste a beautiful day inside."

Sandy placed two cups on the kitchen table and pointed out the window.

"It is a gorgeous day.'

"That breakfast was very good. Thank you. If I keep

eating like that, I will become fat old woman quickly." She patted her stomach.

"I doubt that." A whistle from the teakettle alerted Sandy. "The water's ready." Sandy slipped her hand into a potholder and returned to the table. She poured water into each cup, and they dunked teabags.

"Tawnya, I want to apologize for my questioning the other day."

"Is no need to apologize."

"I was too direct and rude. I still say I'm sorry."

"I like the directness. I despise when people disguise true meaning. With you I know immediately what you think. Is refreshing to me." She took a sip of tea.

"Remember we talked about emotions the other night after the deer hunt? Would you be comfortable with telling me a bit more about your background? I will not judge or condemn you in anything. I think it might help me understand your situation and help you better deal with things. I've had training in this. I think I can help."

Tawnya fingered her teacup and looked at Sandy for a moment.

"I am reluctant to do this for several reasons. Nothing to do with you. What if I cannot find proper emotion? What if my story hardens your heart toward me?"

"I've been around Matt for over twenty years. We've had many conversations about his grief and finding his true emotion. Also, Rich coming back from a combat zone, taking lives and trying to come to a sense of peace with himself. We worked through those things."

"I fear my story may be worse than theirs."

"I'm willing to help you. I know you're deep down

a good person. Here we can forgive someone for doing something wrong. We can try if you want that?" Sandy nodded and sat back.

"Yes, I think I would do this. I cannot be an American and shoot the first person who gives me trouble."

Sandy laughed. "That would be against our rules for sure. We'll start slow. Tell me about your childhood."

"I never knew my parents. I was told they died. Orphanages in Russia were run like military camps. Do this, do that. No questions. I rebelled and received punishment often. No food, when cold outside they would take my blanket away. I had to suppress anger, not allowed to cry. They sent me to different camps to break me."

"How did you handle the anger?"

"Is like computer file. I stash it away. When I am by myself, I let it go, maybe punch something. I learned that something soft is better than something hard to punch." She made a fist.

"That's good. What about school?"

"We studied all day. I used it to escape. I read everything I could. They found out that my worst punishment is taking away a book. The only way I could receive encouragement was to excel in classes. That was my secret. I loved to learn."

"I like that you're using some humor in conversations. It's a good sign."

"Before I came to America, I seldom laughed. Nothing was funny."

"I'm sure. More tea?"

"No, I am good."

"Do you feel okay to continue?"

"Is fine. I have never told anyone some of these things. Is…awkward, I think."

"That's natural. Most of us feel awkward talking about personal issues. Let me ask, what makes you happy?"

Tawnya sipped more tea. For a while she drummed her fingers on the table. Then she leaned forward.

"Giraffes."

"Giraffes? Long necked animals."

"Yes." She said it with a snicker.

"How?"

"One of my assignments was to a…eliminate a high-profile Russian oligarch. He owned the zoo in Moscow and his office was across from the giraffe exhibit. I pretended to be a tourist and stood at the fence. As he came out of the building I reached for my weapon and was licked by a baby giraffe. Right on the top of my head. I could not do anything but laugh. And the man got away that time."

"Oh, my goodness. That had to be a hilarious scene."

"The huge eyes of that baby resembled those of the deer I did not shoot the other day. I have been in love with giraffes ever since."

"These are the kinds of things we need to focus on for you, Tawnya. It brings a whole different appearance to your face. A happy one."

"This is good?"

"Yes. We'll concentrate on making your stay here enjoyable. I know one thing that will excite you. The San Francisco Zoo just last month had two births of baby giraffes. We can drive up there and try to see them if you like."

"We could? I am already looking forward to it. This is very nice of you."

"Okay, the boys will be back soon, but we must talk more later. Would you mind if I gave you a hug?"

"A hug?"

"Yes, in my view everyone needs a hug once in a while. Just to solidify our friendship."

"I guess is okay."

They stood and Sandy went over to her. At first Tawnya tentatively wrapped her arms around Sandy's neck. Sandy pulled her closer and rubbed her back. She thought it would be uncomfortable, unnatural. Somehow it was not.

"This is an American hug, Tawnya. We give them to others when we are happy to be around them. Thank you for trusting me with your story."

"I don't know what to say."

"Nothing needs to be said. Anytime you need a hug, I'm here. And we'll talk more. Okay?"

"Yes, I would like that."

The following day Tawnya finished her workout and hurried to her room for a shower. Her stomach growled as she dried off, anticipating breakfast. Physical activity caused her to increase her calory intake. Hiking, her exercise routine, running and riding the horses honed her into tip top shape. Her wound ceased hurting and merely itched occasionally. Not like it did before though.

When she entered the kitchen, Sandy flopped pancakes onto an already huge pile on a platter and waved.

"Good morning, Sandy. What a beautiful day."

"Got that right. Bacon's about done and the guys will be here in a bit. They're mucking the stalls. They'll want a shower to clean up after, so maybe half hour for them to eat. You can go ahead if you like."

"I will wait for them. A glass of juice will do for now." She opened the refrigerator and grabbed the juice carton.

"Since we have some time can we talk more?" Sandy poured a cup of coffee and sat at the kitchen table.

"Sure. What about?" Tawnya sat across from her.

"Nosey me wants to know more about you. Talking things out is helpful, I think."

"Maybe yes, maybe no. I will be reluctant to talk about my job."

"Of course. I'm curious about your training, family, friends. Just how your life progressed."

Tawnya fingered her juice glass. The first talk they had stirred uncomfortable memories. And from day one her handlers had stressed no personal information should ever be offered. She had already gone against that warning.

"I have no family. My parents died before I had any memory of them. I was married once."

"Really?"

"Yes to a soldier for just over a year and a half. He was killed in Syria. Our baby contracted pneumonia and died four months earlier."

"I'm so sorry. We don't have to talk about that if you don't want to."

"Is a part of my life I have dealt with. Thinking back, we were not like a fairy tale marriage. I became pregnant and we married. The baby was my reason for living. When he died, it was like I also died. I focused on the training they put me into."

"You poor dear."

"Such was life. I was not the only one who lost a baby. Three other women did, too. I was able to escape into a deep intensive course of physical and educational activity."

"You shut out the loss and hurt."

"Was the only thing I could do." She shrugged.

"Now as an American you can start over. Find a nice man to settle down and have another baby. Maybe two or more." Sandy laughed.

"Is not possible. As part of my training, they gave me…I do not know the word. I can have no more babies."

"A hysterectomy? Oh my God."

"Yes. They did not want to interrupt my work to have a child. Loss of valuable time."

"That is cruel. I'm sorry, but it makes me mad." Sandy clenched her fists.

"It is what it is. At that point my life became a pure matter of survival. The better I followed their direction, the better my chances for continuing to live."

"Did you have any friends to help you through this?"

"None during training. We regularly tried to kill each other. We would stop just before it happened. Again, we could not afford to lose anyone but often there was a period of recovery to heal wounds."

"How did you handle the loneliness? It must have been excruciating."

"All my life I have basically been alone. I can only rely on myself. Until I met Matt no one had ever helped me. And I did not need it before. Loneliness is my constant companion." Tawnya noticed tears running down Sandy's cheeks.

"Do not be sad for me. I am okay. I can learn more

about myself as you said yesterday. I look forward to it."

"I must say, you have to be the strongest woman I have ever meet. I admire your courage and attitude."

"I would dispute courage. Alongside loneliness is fear. I would never admit to anyone else, but fear is always present. I fight it first, then confront my problem."

"Tawnya the last person to recognize courage is the one who has it. We will talk more, if you want."

"Yes, we will."

"One more thing, I need a hug." Sandy shrugged.

"You gave me one yesterday, today I give you one back."

This time the embrace was mutual.

Tawnya and Sandy talked twice more in the next few days. Sandy had never encountered anyone like Tawnya. In college she'd majored in education with a minor in psychology. None of the abnormal cases in her studies even came close to this woman. Her heart ached for her, and she hoped and prayed that with her help, Tawnya could become a whole person. And above all a happy and content American.

Chapter 19

Sasha steered the latest SUV rental down the street in Coeur d'Alene looking for the first place they had located Tawnya. A bed and breakfast he remembered.

"There it is. That one on the hill. The gray one."

"These people rent out their home to tourists for money?" Dimitri bent down in the passenger seat to get a better view out Sasha's window.

"They charge large amounts of money for this."

"What do we know about Tawnya's stay here?"

"Was searching for work and moved out after only two days. Do not know where she moved to. But the man she was at restaurant with, also stayed here."

"Who was he?"

"I do not know. But he was the driver who she escaped with." Sasha shrugged.

"Do you think she is still with him?"

"Is my guess. They did not appear to be lovers. Never saw them hold hands or kiss. But he was the reason we do not have her."

"Then we find this man and determine what he knows. Maybe Tawnya is with him. We kill two birds with one pebble. You go find where he lives."

Sasha parked a block away and climbed out of the car.

"Be back soon. With information."

He turned and walked briskly down the street.

Conscious of not drawing attention to himself he kept his head down and eyes focused ahead. He climbed the steps and opened the front door. A woman in the back yelled, "Be right with you."

Soon she entered the hallway and approached the lobby.

"Yes sir, what can we do for you?"

"I have a friend who was staying here a few days ago, and I missed meeting with him. We had business to transact, and I need to find where he lives." Sasha exhibited his best grin.

"I'm sorry but I can't help you. Our guests like to keep that information confidential."

"Oh, I understand but this is critical. The man's name was Matt, and I must have his address, please." His expression hardened. He reached into his pocket and fingered his knife.

"As I said I am not at liberty to give out any addresses."

Sasha pulled out his knife and jabbed it into the wall next to where the woman stood. To her credit she did not yell but jumped and held her hands together in front of her, shaking.

"I am not one to waste time. Two things can happen. One you give me the address and I leave with no damage done to your property or your person, or, well, you do not want to know what number two is." He leaned toward her and wrenched the knife out of the wall.

"Just a minute." She eased over to a cabinet and opened a drawer, pulling out a ledger.

"Just write out the address on a piece of paper and we can pretend this never took place." He leered at her.

She did that and handed him the note.

"A great pleasure having our conversation, Mrs." He left and hurried back to the car.

"Gentlemen, we are off to California."

"What happened in there?" asked Dmitri.

"Got the address of the man."

"Anyone hurt?"

"No, I could not be sure if anyone else was around, so I just left. And I suggest we quickly do the same.

He jumped in and they left minutes before a police car with lights flashing careened down the street and stopped at the Log Inn.

The SUV headed back to Spokane for another plane ride.

Chapter 20

Tawnya reined in at the barn and led her horse inside. She removed the saddle and walked Goldie, a rescued mustang, her favorite of Matt's horses, around to cool down. She brushed the horse as she nuzzled Tawnya. Matt appeared in a rush at the door and waved at her.

"We need to meet in the dining room. Right now." He was out of breath from his run to the barn.

"I will put Goldie in her stall and be there in just a minute."

"Okay." He turned and ran toward the bunkhouse.

Tawnya led the horse inside his stall, slipped a carrot into Goldie's mouth, and headed for the house.

Sandy sat at the dining room table peeling potatoes.

"Hi, Tawnya. What's goin' on?"

"I do not know. Matt called a meeting." She went to the kitchen and brought back a knife. She grabbed a potato and deftly peeled it.

"If there's gonna be a meeting, we'll need coffee. I'll make a pot." Sandy scrambled to the kitchen.

Soon Matt and Rich sat at the table with them.

"Bad news I'm afraid. I just got a call from the owner of the Log Inn Bed and Breakfast in Coeur d'Alene. She just had an unpleasant visit by a Russian who threatened her. They got my address from her."

"Was she hurt?" Sandy's eyes widened.

"No, they just wanted to know where they could find me. Afraid they may have guessed that Tawnya is here or at least they intend to find out if I know where you are. Okay, we had an inkling this might happen. We need to tighten our security."

"I just need a rifle. That is all." Tawnya slapped the table.

"We don't know how many are coming. At least two Susan saw. I'm guessing there was at least one more, besides a driver, probably another one or two. So, we have four or five on the way. They could be here tomorrow."

"Yeah, I'm figuring they will fly here and check out the ranch. If it was me, I'd watch for a day or two to determine the routine and how many people are here." Rich blew out a breath.

"Agreed. Sandy, I'd like you to get a hotel room in San Jose and stay for a few days."

"Not on your life. This is my home, too, and I'm stayin'. I can shoot."

"No, you can't. These are professionals. They will be soldiers and I don't want to have to worry about you. You can stay only, and I mean only, if you go to the safe room when I tell you. Immediately with no hesitation. Are we clear on that?" Matt stared at Sandy.

"Okay. I can prepare some meals ahead of time, so we don't have to scrounge around for food." Sandy nodded.

"Good. Rich, we need to set up cameras and a couple of welcome surprises for them."

"Well, that will just tickle me to no end. We'll figure out the best place for maximum results. I love it. Haven't had a good skirmish for years. Do we involve the police?"

"Tawnya is not yet legally an American citizen, and her documentation is not official. We can't take the chance on alerting the police. And this far out it would be California Highway Patrol and they have limited resources. Especially lacking in high powered weaponry. Afraid we're on our own.

"I've given Riley and Joe a week off. They didn't even ask why, just packed, and skedaddled. They'll be safe. All right. First thing tomorrow we prepare."

"I am sorry I have brought this to your home. I should have left two days ago." Tawnya sighed.

"And where would you go?" Rich asked.

"I don't want anyone hurt or killed. This would be my worst fear. Please just let me go tomorrow."

"Tawnya, they're already coming. It's too late. Besides this is the best circumstance. They don't know what to expect. We'll give them a harsh welcome they won't forget. Look at it this way. You will be helping us out."

"I still am upset that they know where we are."

"Little lady, they're gonna wish they'd just turned around and trotted back to Moscow." Rich's grin threatened to swallow his face.

"For the next few days, Tawnya, I think you should stay inside. They don't know for sure you're here and we should keep it that way. Rich and I will make trips to the other buildings to take care of the horses and do other chores. And we should wear different clothes and hats to make them think there are more on the ranch than just us." Matt swallowed some coffee and tried to think of anything else that needed to be done.

"What if they have night vision and they attack after

dark?" Rich asked.

"Good point. We need to each carry out tach flashlights with fresh batteries. And Rich, one of us should be on watch at night. And we take a nap when we can. I'll take tonight."

"I'll take care of the flashlights. Just bought some batteries three days ago. And there are Tach lights in the weapons room for all of us. I'll get 'em first thing tomorrow."

Sandy snapped her fingers. "Almost forgot, any time you're hungry there's a bag of protein bars that I'll set on the kitchen table and the freezer will have microwaveable mini meals soon as I fix 'em. If they cut the power, the safe room has its own generator and microwave."

"Sounds like our plan is set. Any questions?" Matt looked at each of them. Three heads shook. "Now we prepare and wait. Tomorrow will be a busy day."

Chapter 21

The call from Susan, the Bed and Breakfast owner, gave Matt a headache. Now the Russians knew where he lived, and he had no doubt they were on their way. He needed to set up security, go over a plan to react to an attack with Rich, and ensure everyone knew the seriousness of this latest news.

The wind whistled through the scrub bush along his path. The chirping of the birds flittering back and forth suggested a peaceful time. That won't last long. How are we going to survive an onslaught of KGB killers? Yes, they'd prepared. But was it enough?

Tawnya would be an asset and so would Rich. His ranch hands, Riley and Joe, not so much. Excellent men with livestock and ranch chores, but in an assault, they would be liabilities. Best that he gave them a couple of days off. Sandy would be hidden in the safe room, so he wouldn't have to worry about her.

Matt stared at the mountains surrounding his ranch. Yes, his ranch now that his parents were gone. They'd had such big plans for him. Taking over after his father retired from his Silicon Valley software company. Grooming Matt for a CEO career had been John Pearson's sole goal in a life, cut short all too soon.

Two and a half years now. How could it be that long? He'd never learned to properly grieve for his mom and dad. What are the rules and guidelines when your parents are killed on a side trip from a Mexican cruise? No siblings remained to lean on or share.

No one had been identified as responsible for their deaths. Gruesome details of the condition of the bodies when discovered fluttered through his mind. Desolation and solitude had replaced the anger that boiled up when he'd learned their fate.

Then his fiancée's sudden death threw another monkey wrench at him. He needed to work through that as well.

He shook his head. Need to deal directly with these things. He'd tried therapy. For him a waste of money. That was not a worry. He'd reaped several lifetimes of wealth from the sale of the business. Never a fan of sitting at a desk, crunching numbers, or directing board meetings, Matt wanted to be active, interact with people, fly his plane, do something to help someone. Live. His talks with Sandy had helped. She had a way of straightening out the confusing and unsettling thoughts he dealt with.

When these depressing thoughts grabbed his attention, the mountains also helped comfort him. The way the geologic composition of the Diablo Range provided the sun an easel to craft pink and lavender coatings soothed and quieted his discontent. Magical indeed and he missed that connection when he left.

Matt continued his early morning walk to his favorite view. The entire valley spread out in front of him. He and Sharon had spent several hours sitting here planning their life together. Only to be replaced with more grief and despair a few months ago.

The ranch sitting in this corner, and a vast field of grass spotted with his cattle and horses stretched for four miles to the opposite foothills. A tributary of the Guadalupe split the valley and marked the natural boundary of the northeast side of Rancho Elaine.

This visit's second purpose captured his attention. Where would attackers have an advantage in an ambush? As a working ranch, the areas around the buildings had been cleared. No one in his family had spent time nurturing flowers or vegetation to beautify the place. Too many other things needed attention on a working ranch.

The road leading through a natural pass ended at the ranch house. Just beyond the four outbuildings sat in a line angling northeast. Hard dirt comprised the makeup of the grounds and gravel rock provided pathways to each building. The corral occupied a large area north of the stable, the last of the outbuildings.

Off to Matt's right the top of a hillside featured flat enough boulder-strewn cover for a sniper. The same scenario appeared to Matt's left. Tree cover and elevation would give a shooter an uncluttered view of the property. There were four spots of vulnerability. Each of these now contained a video camera and recorder focused on a possible setup for intruders. Matt attached the tiny camera on a tall sapling and flipped the switch.

"That's the last one, Rich. How do they look?" Matt held his hand to his earpiece.

"Good for me. Got a wide coverage area on all four."

"It's amazing how small these things are and the resolution they provide."

"American engineering's best, my man. These new ones are as good as those I had in Iraq."

"How we doin' on the booby traps?"

"I suggest we all avoid the tree area to the left of the road. And do not take a straight track up the East hill where you are."

"Copy that. Everyone been advised?"

"Done. Tawnya was a big help setting them up. I'd say she's not inexperienced."

"I leave that to you guys. Never liked to play with things that could blow me up."

Chapter 22

The four KGB operatives located a motel within two miles of the address they had been given. After a quick early breakfast, they gathered in Pietor and Sasha's room to plan their attack. They had hauled in two bags of equipment and set about checking their weapons. Six rifles, six pistols with holsters, twelve magazines of ammunition, a dozen grenades, four tactical knives, bottles of water and packs of protein bars lay on one of the twin beds.

Each man claimed a rifle and handgun, ejected magazines, and then clicked them back in place. Filling their pockets with bars, bottles of water, extra ammo, each one chose a knife and geared up. No one spoke amid the noise of the racking of equipment. Once done, they spread out on the other bed and in the lone desk chair. Pietor remained standing and one by one focused on each man's face.

"Brothers, we have an important job to do. It will be easy if we work together and follow our plan. A few minutes ago, I talked to Gregor to be sure of our task. He expects us to capture Tawnya if she is here. If she is not, we find out where she is and go get her.

"He wants her alive. I have drugs to administer that will keep her docile all the way to Russia." He patted his breast pocket. "If, and hear this, if there is no other option, we eliminate her and bring the body back. This is worst case possibility only."

"How do we make it back to Russia?" Dimitri shifted his holster to keep it from jabbing his stomach.

"The plane that brought us here is still at the San Jose airport in a private hanger. We travel to New York and transfer to overseas Ilyushin-76 to fly to Saint Petersburg."

"Will be difficult to haul around a body and pass the customs inspection."

"Gregor has purchased a coffin. It will be on the plane. We put Tawnya in it whether she is dead or just drugged. Time difference is eleven hours. She will be given enough to keep her sedated. We will become an honor guard to bring our dear departed back home."

All of them emitted sighs of relief.

"Gregor is smart man. Thinks of everything." Pietor chuckled.

"I wish we had night vision equipment. Do not like to do this in daylight." Symon Koval absently scratched his beard stubble.

"Was not possible to obtain on short notice. We will do fine. Are we not Spetsnaz? Today we will only observe. We finalize our plan and tomorrow early, we finish our task."

****

Pietor forced his binoculars deeper into his eyes trying to better identify the man in his view walking to one of the buildings. They'd been watching the ranch house for the last two hours spread out in the hills eight hundred to one thousand meters away. The early morning sun splashed the valley in bright light and heavy shadows. Sasha, off to his left hiding in thick bushes, checked the other buildings. Symon Koval crawled along the hill to his right. He could not see Dmitri Oborin.

"How many do you see, Sasha?" He pressed his ear buds tightly.

"Four men so far. One in the far building, I think is the barn. Later one man unloading a pickup. I think hay. Another one walking to the second building. Shorter than the first man. Could be Tawnya dressed in men's clothes. About her height but heavier. Hard to tell. Face is in shadows. Never clear."

"Same here. Baseball caps on everyone. Five different caps but they could just be the same person wearing different ones each time they go out. Clothing was different also. My guess is four or five men. If one is Tawnya, that makes four men and her. No way to be positive."

Back at their motel, they compared notes to determine if they needed to adjust their plan.

"We will capture one of those men and find out if she is there. This afternoon two hours before the sun sets, we will do more surveillance. Sasha will choose one of them who is by himself and capture him. After all these are just farmers."

"What if she is not here?" Symon guzzled a soda.

"We tell Gregor and let him determine next move. Right now, we will assume she is here, or we find out where she is and go there. Simple." Pietor ran his hand through scraggly brown hair.

"The other people in the ranch? What happens to them?" Sasha, in a bit of overkill, for the second time in two days cleaned his rifle.

"No witnesses left alive. Make it appear to be gang

fight or fight over drugs. Everyone clear?"

They all nodded.

"We have…" He glanced at his watch. "Six hours. We find some food and then get some sleep. We will be up late tonight."

"I do not see it. Wait. There it is. Dirt road off to the right. I almost missed it. Go." Pietor pointed a few meters ahead. The SUV turned and followed up an incline on a dirt path, barely a road.

"Stop before we get to the top. I will check for traffic."

As the car lurched to a stop, he leaped out and jogged up to the pass between to hills. He crouched behind some scrub brush, then waved them forward. He opened the door and jumped inside.

"Park over behind those trees where we were before. They will hide the vehicle."

They opened the hatch and emptied their gear bags. Weapons, ammunition, protective vests, and backpacks all secured. The four camouflaged men branched out and proceeded down the road. Sasha went left to a copse of trees, Pietor right behind two truck-sized boulders to set up a sniper sight. Symon weaved from bush to tree to bush for cover beside the road leading to the ranch. Dmitri moved parallel to Symon on the right side of the road. Both dove flat on the ground behind bramble bushes for cover, rifles at the ready.

"Radio check. Report." Pietor tapped his ear buds.

"Clear." Three responses.

"Observe and report. Find adequate cover." Pietor double checked his rifle. A downed tree next to the largest boulder proved to be a perfect rest for his new

Chukavin sniper rifle chambered in 7.62x54R. He crouched and peered through the high-resolution telescopic sight. Ideal spot with a wide view of the ranch. No movement. No vehicles parked anywhere. Maybe deserted.

"Anyone see anything?"

"Only some wolf scat I just kneeled in." Sasha cursed.

"Probably was coyote and you get to ride in the back when we leave." Pietor laughed.

"Not funny. Got it on my hands too. Ugh."

"I want to drive. No longer in the back seat. Please?" Symon chimed in.

"Settle down. We have a task to complete. Hold positions and report any activity." Pietor clicked his mic twice, their signal to cease chatter.

Chapter 23

Matt sat at his command center desk. Two seventeen-inch monitors displayed almost ninety percent of the area around the ranch buildings. Rich, Sandy, and Tawnya perched on folding chairs, looking over his shoulder.

The first contact occurred yesterday. Four men stayed up in the hills watching ranch activity. Earlier today the four came closer but spread out in the hills. Camera Two by the big boulders showed movement around the downed tree limb. Rich had identified it as a perfect sniper spot. Camera One revealed two men laying in the bushes on either side of the road. And the fourth sitting on the ground in the trees on the hill to the right of the ranch house. All were armed with rifles. All wore black camouflage grease on their faces. Hard to identify.

Matt and Rich had made several trips around the ranch yesterday and that morning wearing different clothes each time to confuse their watchers. Whoever was walking outside had radio contact with the person manning the camera access to alert them to any hostile activity.

Tawnya had stayed inside. The gray SUV the men had arrived in had been parked twice yesterday and once today dead in front of the tree containing Camera Five positioned to view the access road.

"Okay, here's what I think. They spent time as we figured checking the layout. Not spotting Tawnya they're not sure if she's here. That leaves an attack to either capture one of us for interrogation, or to gain access inside to determine if she's here."

"Do we wait for them to fire the first shot?" Rich growled.

"We can't just take them out. What if we're wrong and they aren't the guys Susan told us about?" Matt shrugged.

"They are Russians. I can tell by the way they move. Spetsnaz." Tawnya slapped her hands together. "Shoot them."

"If they are they will attack soon if they don't have night vision capability. If they do have it, I'm guessing around midnight or later. We keep our weapons close. Right now, we monitor and wait."

"I have our night vision gear in the kitchen. Flashlights there, too. Ready just in case." Rich nodded toward the kitchen.

"Good," Matt said.

"The guy to the right of the road is about twenty feet from one of my surprise packages. And the one in the trees almost sat on one. If he moves two feet left, show time. Another one is in a direct line from the boulder down the hill."

"Got it. We watch them on the monitor. When they move, so do we." Matt checked his watch. "Just past five p.m. Won't be long. Sandy, best you head to the safe room. Lock yourself in. The setup in there will let you view the rooms of the ranch and the front porch area. Grab some of that food you fixed for us."

"I don't like leaving this lay. I still say I could

help." She frowned.

"We all feel better not having to worry about you. Now git."

"Sandy, let me give you hug." Tawnya rushed over to her, and they embraced.

"Do not worry. I will protect Matt for you." She whispered in Sandy's ear.

"Thank you. Be safe." Sandy replied.

Then Sandy turned and headed to the safe room. She looked back when she reached the door. "I'll say some prayers for all of you. God be with you." Then she was gone.

The room grew quiet as they waited.

"I can see that the three men down closer to us have rifles. I'm certain the guy by the rocks has a sniper rifle. Don't see any night vision headsets. Wish I had my drone from Iraq. Would come in real handy." Rich laughed.

A half hour later Rich finished his third lap around the room.

"Been thinkin'. Why are they here? We believe they're looking for Tawnya and they're not sure if she's here. As a former on-the-ground platoon leader my next move would be to capture one of us for interrogation. Am I right?"

"Yes. Is logical. I too have thought this." Tawnya sighed.

"So why don't we let them?"

"Let them what?" Matt looked over his shoulder.

"Capture one of us." Rich opened his hands.

"That's nuts."

"I will do it." Tawnya raised her hand.

"No. I will. I'm the best one here for hand-to-hand

combat. They will want to question me. I won't let 'em." Rich gave them all a stare.

"That's insane. It could get you killed or at least wounded. No. Let's wait." Matt turned back to the computers.

"Right now, we're in a stalemate. I for one would rather have something happen now instead of after dark. We have visuals with the cameras. They're pinpointed. Our advantage. Think about it."

Matt turned back. What Rich said made sense as far as working in the daylight. But Rich was also thirty-three percent of their offense. They couldn't afford to lose anyone.

"Trust me, Matt. I can do this."

"I think is best plan." Tawnya made a fist.

"Let's talk this out. Where would you go to do this?"

"Not the barn because of the animals. Not where the extra weapons are. I'd say the ATV storage shed. Like I'm getting one ready to use. Plenty of maneuvering room in there." Rich scratched his head.

"What's your plan once you're captured?"

"Watch for my opportunity and take the guy down."

"I still think it's crazy. But your point about doing this in the daylight makes a lot of sense. If they get you, I'm guessing they'll send another guy to help. What then?" Matt shook his head.

"Then I get to take out two of them. Odds switch to our favor."

"Yes. This makes tactical advantage possible." Tawnya chambered a round in the rifle she'd picked up.

"Okay. Against my better judgement we do this. I'm relying on your field experience, Rich. And Tawnya's. Head back here when you finish. The back way. You'll have to first go out front so they can see where you're going."

"I'll leave my rifle here. Just have my Glock and a knife."

"Just don't get yourself killed."

"Not in my plans, my friend. Not in my plans."

"Give it about ten minutes and go." Matt checked his watch.

Rich laid his rifle on the kitchen table, took off his holster and placed the pistol at his back under his belt. That table was covered with various weapons. All recently cleaned and loaded. Matt hoped they wouldn't need all of them.

Ten minutes later Rich exited the front door and walked down the road to the second building north of the ranch house. Matt watched as the one of the men at the side of the road rose to a kneeling position. He watched Rich till he went inside. Then he moved from cover to cover edging closer to where Rich had disappeared.

"He's on your tail, Rich. Fifty yards behind. The other men are staying put. He's all yours, buddy." Matt clicked off.

"Got it."

Swinging the door of the shed open, Rich entered and didn't close the door. He turned on the inside lights and moved to the first of four ATVs. He lifted a toolbox from a shelf and opened the vehicle's hood. He tapped the motor with a wrench to pretend to be working on it.

He didn't hear the man enter but felt the barrel of a rifle at his back.

"Do not move. Who are you?" A man just a bit shorter than him dressed in camo spoke. He had grease smeared on his face and handled the rifle competently, like it was another limb.

"I'm a ranch hand. Just a nobody. What's this about?"

"Turn around, slowly. I ask questions. Not you. How many are here?"

"Let's see. There's Bill, and Tom, Greg, and his son Steve. So, I guess with me, Five."

"Who is the woman?" The gun never wavered.

"No woman. The ladies are out shopping." Rich lifted his hands.

"Put down the wrench." The man said something in Russian.

"Sorry, I don't understand. What do you want?"

"Shut up. I am listening." He pressed one hand to his ear.

The man's eyes veered away for a second. Just what Rich had been waiting for. He jumped forward swatting the rifle barrel away and clocked him with the wrench. The thud resounded through the room as the man slumped to the floor.

Rich hadn't wanted to hit him that hard, but it was too late to try again. He felt for a pulse. He found none. He pulled the man farther inside and searched him. Nothing, not even a wallet. He removed the earbuds, grabbed the rifle, and hurried out the back door. Two minutes later he was back in the command center.

He handed the buds to Tawnya and reported to Matt what had happened.

"Good job, Rich. Guess I shouldn't have doubted you. Tawnya, let us know what they're saying." Matt studied the monitors.

"Nothing yet. Did the man yell when you hit him?"

"No. The only sound was the wrench thunking him."

"Matt, do you want me to answer them if they call?" She asked.

"No. They don't know you're here yet. Let's keep 'em in the dark. Just let us know what they are saying."

"Okay. Odds now even." She grinned.

Chapter 24

Symon watched the man leave the house and head north. Maybe this is the one he could take to get answers. The man opened a door to the third building and went inside. And he left the door open. Nice.

"Pietor, I will capture that man and find out if Tawnya is here."

"Good. Be careful."

"Is only a cowboy and he has no six-shooter." Symon laughed.

"Still take care. We want him alive to talk."

"As they say here, piece of cake. Chocolate is my favorite." Symon chuckled as he crouched and moved from sparse cover to sparse cover.

He waited at the door and then moved in the opening. The man seemed to be working on an ATV parked near the front. Symon crept up and stuck his rifle into the man's back.

"Do not move. Who are you?"

The man hesitated. "I'm a ranch hand. Just a nobody. What's this about?"

"Turn around, slowly. I ask questions. Not you. How many are here?"

"Let's see. There's Bill, and Tom, Greg, and his son Steve. So, I guess with me, Five."

"Who is the woman?"

"No woman. The ladies are out shopping." The man

lifted his hands.

"Put down the wrench." In Russian he told Pietor he had the man.

"Sorry, I don't understand. What do you want?" the man asked.

"Shut up. I am listening." Symon pressed one hand to his ear. The transmission was garbled. Suddenly his rifle pointed away and a silver object flew toward his head. Then nothing.

Pietor settled back and waited for Symon to finish his interrogation. Hopefully Tawnya is here, they could grab her and be back on a plane headed home within a few hours. Five months. It had been five months since he had been home. Two assassinations and a two-month trek across Bulgaria in the middle of winter had taxed his body.

He longed to be home with his wife, Natalia. She was his latest woman. A model from Belarus who loved caviar. He would need to stop somewhere to get some. Was very easy to please her. He hoped she was still at his home.

A grunt in his ear snapped him out of his reverie. He waited for Symon to say something. Probably having to inflict punishment to get answers. Symon was best at interrogation.

"Symon?" No answer.

"Symon? Copy?" Pietor began to worry.

"Dmitri do you have Symon in sight?"

"No. He went inside five minutes ago. Can not see inside. Too dark."

"Go check on him, Dmitri."

"On it."

Dmitri repeated Symon's approach to the building.

151

He stopped short of the door, trying to see deeper inside.

"Going in." Dmitri clicked.

"Pietor, Symon is down. Dead from blow to the head. What do we do?"

"Sasha, what do you see at the ranch?"

"Nothing, is quiet. I will move closer…"

The explosion reverberated through the hills. Pietor gasped as Sasha's body was thrown into the air. What is going on?

"Dmitri, check on Sasha. Leave Symon."

"On my way."

Dmitrii scrambled back to the road and wove his way through the trees Sasha had settled in. Limbs whipped his face as he crashed through. Then he found him.

"Sasha is gone too. Looks like a trap. IED. His left leg and left arm are gone. Enough of this." Dmitri threw down his backpack and took out all four grenades. He rushed down toward the house and lofted two at the front door. He held the third armed grenade back ready to throw when his head exploded in a mist of pink.

Pietor enraged that a couple of simple farmers had eliminated his team, began firing at the house. Movement inside prompted him to attack on his own. He could take them. He would do it for his men.

Rich rolled back from the window where he'd stopped the grenade attacker. Bullets spattered the foyer and blasted the front window. A sudden breeze allowed the curtains to flutter wildly inside. He moved back to the dining room. Tawnya stood at the table with a rifle in her hand.

"Three down and one left. He is mine. Keep his attention to the front of the house. I will go out the back and get up the hill." She headed to the back door.

"Good luck. Yell if you need help." Rich waved.

Rich couldn't chance standing at a window. The shells the sniper was using were tearing up the inside. All he could do was move from window to window and shake the curtains. The house had five windows facing the hill. Each had a set of curtains that Rich shook and still stayed out of sight.

Chapter 25

Tawnya left the ranchhouse out the back door and angled around the stable. She carried the rifle Matt had put into her hands. He had nodded at her and wished her well, telling her the weapon had been tested and would be zeroed in. Also, her heavy gun loaded with thirteen hollow point bullets flapped reassuringly in the holster at her side.

Up the hill on the far side the trees provided plenty of cover. She would attempt to approach from the shooter's back side. She felt good as she jogged up the terrain, careful to avoid the marked trees Rich had coached her on to bypass the explosives. Finally, she felt one hundred percent. Workouts here had been just what she needed to regain her strength and stamina and heal.

The sniper still fired at any movement at the ranch not yet aware of her ascent. Tawnya remembered previous hunts through similar hillsides. Some in Europe mirrored those here. The reports of the sniper's rifle directed her up a steeper incline. Rocks tumbled down as she climbed higher. She stopped.

Closer now she tried to locate his position. Still too far away. As she crouched down, a puff of dirt inches away from her head exploded. He had her targeted. She rolled and another puff erupted in front of her. She now lost her footing and began a slide down. Cuts and bumps from rocks, trees, and bushes slapping at her made the descent painful. Fortunately, she did not lose her grip on the rifle.

She came to a stop at a downed limb and hurriedly dove over it. A bullet impacted the limb exactly where she had been. She rested the rifle's barrel between branches of the limb and scanned the hillside. It was never beneficial to be the down target on a hillside. She thought a movement in a shadow might be the shooter. He had stopped shooting, so she was not able to pinpoint his location.

She waited. Nothing happened. One of them would have to make a move. Waiting was second nature to snipers. And she was one of Russia's best. The top of the hill she attempted to climb showed around five hundred yards through her scope. She was glad the sun shone on the other side of the hill so her metal would not flash in the sunlight.

She crawled down to the end of the limb and replaced her rifle on top. Still waiting. Bruises and cuts stabbed at her from myriad parts of her body. Somehow, they seemed a familiar part of her stalk. How many times had she been in this situation? Too many to count.

At last, she spotted the man. It was Pietor. He rose from behind a bush and jogged toward the rise. She aimed and willed herself to be steady. The gun jerked and Pietor stumbled. His head swiveled back at her as he fell and dropped his rifle.

She hurried up the hill, her rifle in a steady grip in front of her. Scrabbling up as fast as she could, it seemed to take forever. Pietor lay on his back where he had fallen, blood quickly spreading on his chest just above his protective vest. Here was her nemesis all these years. From her first indoctrination as a spy, he was there.

Competing, attempting to outdo each other in everything.

Tawnya kicked his rifle away and stood over him, pointing her rifle at his chest.

He nodded. "Good shot. You were always the best." He choked back a gasp.

Obviously, the wound was severe. She placed her rifle on the ground several feet away from him, bent down and took off her sweater, stuffing it on his wound. He was someone she knew, in an awkward way had grown up with, and she could not just stand and watch him without trying to help.

"Here hold this tight. I will call for help." She mashed the sweater down hard. He held it over the wound as she reached for her phone.

"Tawnya, are you okay? We heard shots." Matt's voice radiated concern.

"I am fine. Pietor has been wounded. It is bad. We are at the summit just to the side of the road. He needs help."

"Be right there. Is he a threat?"

"No just wounded."

"Tawnya no need to call. It is very bad. I feel it." Pietor groaned.

"Do not talk. Save your strength. We will get you to a hospital." She shoved her phone into a pocket and worked feverishly trying to stop the bleeding.

"Then what. A prison. No, I will die here." He spoke softly, carefully it appeared.

"Why do you think I did not kill you in New York?" He spat blood. "I had every chance. Do not think badly of me, my dear Tawnya. You never knew my secret. Our secret."

"What are you talking about?"

Pietor coughed and winced. Blood continued to ooze from his chest wound around Tawnya's hands.

"Remember when we trained, and…it seemed like I was given special treatment?"

"It made me furious. I hated you."

"It came from the top. President Malinova. I am his son. This I discovered only recently. Gregor kept it from us." Pain etched on his face caused him to flinch. He gulped and coughed once more.

"That explains much."

"It does not explain why I spared you. Is not my only secret."

"I frankly do not care about your secrets."

"Oh, this one you will. You are my sister…I only wish I could have told you before. I could not kill my flesh and blood."

"This cannot be. I am the daughter of that monster?"

"Yes. I have one favor to ask before I die."

"We can get help for you." She pressed harder on his chest.

"It will not be in time…Please let me rest in Russia…I want to go back home. Please?"

"I will never set foot in Russia again. I am assigned a death warrant there. How could I do this?"

"Will you try, my sister?" He placed his hand on hers. "I wish things would have been different…I always felt bad about not having a brother or sister…Family is not important to those in control in Russia."

Tawnya looked down at her brother and felt a twinge. "I will try. Yes, I will."

Pietor groaned and breathed a last breath.

She sighed. In an instant a brother found and then

lost. Such is my life.

Ten minutes later the chug of Matt's ATV disrupted Tawnya's attempt to identify the birds chirping away now that the gunfire had ceased. Matt pulled up alongside Tawnya and jumped out.

"Everything okay?" His eyes searched the hillside, and his rifle barrel followed his scan.

"Is good. Meet my brother." She pointed to the body lying under a tall oak.

"Your brother? For real?' He lowered his weapon.

"That is what he said. Seems we were both in the dark about our heritage. He told me our parents are Mr. and Mrs. Malinova."

"Sheeit. The Russian president?" Matt couldn't interpret the look on Tawnya's face.

"As you cowboys say, yep."

"We need to sit down and think about ramifications. The whole Russian Army could be headed this way. We're good, but not that good."

"Help me get Pietor on the back of the ATV and let's get back. Is Rich all right?"

"Yep, the other three are done for."

They placed Pietor on the back where many animal carcasses had rested. This was the first human remains it had carried. Silence between them on the ride back was spent contemplating what to do next. They rode past the ranch house on to the stable where Rich stood as if guarding the bodies sprawled on the ground.

"Hey, Tawnya. I see you collected one for yourself." Rich smiled.

"Rich, let's haul these guys into the barn. We may not be done yet." Matt pulled the body off the ATV and dragged it toward the doorway.

Rich shrugged and did the same with the legs of two of the other bodies. Tawnya took the last one. They made a trail of scuffed dirt all the way inside. Matt spread a tarpaulin out and they piled the men on top in the corner.

They gathered outside and Rich drug his sleeve across his forehead to wipe away the sweat.

"What's going on? More guys comin'?"

"We need to talk. Inside please."

Tawnya turned and headed to the ranch house.

"She'll explain. Lots more to the story."

They sat at the dining table with iced tea sitting in front of them. Sandy had joined them and had not said a word. The looks on their faces probably told her something was up.

Tawnya launched into a recap of her life. From her early years, academics, training, and eventually her becoming a spy. When she detailed her assignments, not all of them, Rich held up his hand.

"Don't know about you folks, but I need something stronger than tea. Anyone else?"

Matt and Sandy's hands shot up quickly. Rich got up and returned with a six pack of beer. He also had a bottle of Vodka and a glass for Tawnya. He handed a beer to Matt and Sandy and the glass to Tawnya.

"Picked up a bottle while I was in town yesterday. I know you're not a fan of beer." He spoke to Tawnya.

"I thank you, so thoughtful." She twisted off the cap and poured two fingers into the glass. She raised it up. "Cheers."

They drank. Then Tawnya continued her tale.

"The man I shot on the hill was Pietor Abramov. We grew up together, went through the same training and were sent on our different assignments. I never liked him. He was an arrogant, sexist pig as far as I was concerned. Also very competent, an expert in weapons, martial arts, almost anything he attempted. He attacked me in New York after breaking into my apartment.

"They sent him to take me back to Russia after I decided to quit. On the hill as he was dying, he told me he was my brother. Our father is Alexander Malinova. He just found out himself recently. We never knew."

"Holy crap! What a turn of events." Rich guzzled half his beer.

"How do you feel about that?" Sandy was wide-eyed.

Tawnya looked at her. "I do not know. This thing about feelings is foreign to me. All my training forced us to eliminate feelings. They could get you killed. Therefore, I have a difficult time identifying them.

"When I shot him, I knew it was him or me. I guess satisfaction at succeeding is what I felt. Then when he told me I was his sister, I no longer felt satisfied. Not exactly sad but not happy either. I will need to study more about feelings and maybe learn how to recognize them. I do not believe I suffer about this, but I lack information to determine how I now must live."

"Tawnya, if there is anything I can do for you, I am here. Anytime, okay?" Sandy's eyes filled with tears. "What a rotten thing to do to a person. I can't imagine." She shook her head.

"I think we all think the same. We're all here for you," Matt said.

"Thank you. Your kindness is very helpful."

"How's the vodka?" Rich asked.

"Tastes like *Samogon*." She eyed the glass.

"What's Samogon?"

"Is Russian moonshine." She laughed.

"Very funny. Tawnya made a joke." Rich grinned.

"Let's talk about the situation. We have four dead bodies out there. Their IDs are obviously fake. We need to find the vehicle they came in and figure out what to do? Can't go to the police. It would jeopardize Tawnya. I doubt any of the neighbors would report the gunfire because we shoot at the range all the time, so that's not a worry." Matt finished his beer.

"Don't worry about their car. It's in the garage. I found it while Tawnya went up the hill. I was coming up the back way to help out. Course, she didn't need it. I saw you come up with the ATV and went ahead and brought the car back." Rich reached over and hoisted another beer. He burped.

"I saw you coming. I almost shot you until I recognized your face," Tawnya said.

"Thanks for that. I would never have forgiven you for killing me." He raised his beer to her. She grinned.

"Which leaves the bodies. What do we do with them?" Matt opened his hands.

"Not a problem Kemo Sabe. Do you not remember my brother has a mortuary, with a fine crematorium?" Rich wiggled his eyebrows.

"Seriously? You want to get him involved?"

"Ain't that what brothers are for? Helpin'?"

"Forgive me, but I have a request. Before Pietor died he asked me to have his ashes taken to Russia for burial. Can we retrieve his ashes?"

"I'm sure we can. They can be put in an urn." Rich nodded.

"How are we going to get them to Russia and where would they be sent?" Matt leaned forward.

"I told you about Gregor. He will not quit searching and coming after me. I will go back and deal with him. This is what I do." Tawnya's paused; her determination clear to everyone.

"No, you can't be serious." Rich grabbed Tawnya's hand. "Please, if you go you won't come back. It's too dangerous and you could die."

"Danger is an old friend. My assignments included danger as an afterthought. I am very good. If I do not eliminate Gregor, I will always have to check my back. He is powerful, has unlimited resources and is like bulldog who will not release his hold. If he is gone then his reports to Malinova will cease. I will be free. This is my only hope."

"I understand what you're saying but I agree with Rich. Too dangerous."

"You do not know me well. There is no alternative, and my mind is made up. I will go."

Matt stared at the woman. No question she was capable, but alone she would have little chance. Determination was written all over her face.

"Only one way we'll let you do this. I'm going with you. I can get transportation for you in and out. I know enough Russian to fake it. I will be your backup."

The next morning a black limousine pulled up to the ranch house. A tall man in a tailored business suit climbed out and walked up the porch stairs. He removed his cowboy hat and smoothed graying brown hair. Before he could knock, Rich opened the door and stepped outside. He slapped the man on the shoulder and ushered him inside.

"Everyone this is my brother, Taylor Garnett. Taylor, you know Sandy. This guy here is Matt and that's

Tawnya." He pointed.

"Hello, Matt. I've heard a lot about you. The few times I've been here, you've been off somewhere traveling. Nice to finally meet you." He shook Matt's hand.

"Can we get you some coffee or something?" Sandy offered.

"I'm okay. Rich was a bit reticent to talk over the phone. You apparently need my services."

"Let's sit in the dining room." They took seats at the table.

Rich spent a few minutes describing the last several hours and Tawnya's situation.

"I have a huge favor to ask. And I, we, understand if you decline. With no hard feelings. The gunfight yesterday resulted in four deaths. KGB killers who wanted to eliminate us. All of us. We would like to use your crematorium to dispose of the bodies. Matt will cover costs. Completely. Only one stipulation is necessary. No paperwork. No record of this is to be made."

Taylor sat back in his chair. He smoothed his thin moustache and paused.

"You know I could lose my license, in fact my business if someone were to find out?" He reached for a handkerchief and wiped his brow.

"Yes, we know the consequences of our request. That's why it's totally up to you."

"What record is there of these men coming here?"

"They arrived by private plane and carried fake IDs. Only the Russians are aware of their attack."

"Forgive me, but why not just bury them in the hills somewhere?"

"One of the men is Tawnya's brother, and she'd like to take his remains back home."

"Big brother, I once told you how much I admired your service and that if you ever needed anything, I'd be there. I guess it's time to honor my promise. Okay, I'll do it. But if I get killed because of this, Mom's gonna be mad at you." Taylor grinned.

"Taylor, that's the scariest part of this whole ordeal."

"For sure."

"We'll help in whatever way we can. Matt has loaded them in the horse trailer, and it's hooked up to the 150. You say the word and we'll bring it to you."

"No, would be too risky. I'll have my horse van come over. It's an official mortuary vehicle. Many ranchers want to cremate a favorite horse and keep the remains. Happens a lot. It'll be here tomorrow, first thing."

"Taylor, I thank you. You send me a bill and pad it however you want." Matt stood and shook his hand.

Taylor left and it seemed they had one less problem to deal with.

Chapter 26

Light traffic greeted them as they pulled out of the rented house's driveway in Saint Petersburg, Russia. Tawnya had proved her worth already. Gaining access to the old house and confiscating a not too old and not too new dark blue Creta four-wheel-drive in a whirlwind twenty-minute episode yesterday made Matt proud. And even more satisfied that Tawnya could handle any situation they would encounter. At least that was the hope.

Their flight from New York to Helsinki gave them time to work out a plan. Thanks to an international pilot friend Matt borrowed the man's forty-foot yacht to navigate the Finland Sea and dock at the port of Saint Petersburg.

Excellent authentic-looking documents identified them as husband and wife from Canada traveling the world in their boat. They informed the customs official that they stopped in Russia to deliver a vase filled with her parent's remains who wanted to be buried in their homeland. She had held out the vase for inspection, but no one wanted to touch it. At midnight they climbed in the car and headed to Gregor's.

"How far is Gregor's home?" Matt studied a map on his cell.

"Not far. Maybe twenty kilometers. I think about twelve miles for you. And you will not find the road on any map."

"Are you sure he'll be there?"

"Is his favorite place. I have been here many times. More than I care to remember. I lived there for over two years. We can hope that he is home." She shuddered.

"I know we need to check out his security, but what about weapons?"

"We can get weapons when we arrive." She grinned. "Not to worry."

"I feel naked without any gear. A knife, knitting needle, something."

"Remember the thorough inspection we went through at customs. They check for metal, electronic equipment, explosives, everything. We could not hope to bring anything into the country. We will be okay. As you say, chill."

"Tawnya, the comedian. Okay, I am chilling."

"Ha. Not possible with you. I have you figured out."

Tawnya turned down a dirt road leading toward the sea. She pulled into a patch of trees and shut the car off. Their bags and the vase were packed inside.

"We walk from here. Two kilometers."

Matt settled in step at a fast pace beside Tawnya, and they used the density of trees as cover to seek out security around Gregor's dacha. They'd been winding through the forest for about twenty minutes when Tawnya held up her fists.

"Just ahead we will come to an open area. There we crawl forward about fifty meters to a berm. Duck behind it and then we can view the grounds. An electric fence surrounds the home. It is guarded by Russian Caucasian wolfhounds and a handler armed with an AK-74."

"And I didn't bring any steak or treats for the dogs.

Or for that matter guns for the handler. Why do I feel like we're gonna die here?"

"Do not worry I will save you." She blinked her eyes at him.

Darkness enveloped them and visibility lessened with each step they took. Matt wished for night vision goggles. He had totally relied on Tawnya's skill set for this mission. His regrets were flying through his brain with each tidbit of knowledge he gained. Fortunately, the moon would be no problem due to an overcast sky. Beyond the berm a bright artificial horizon let them know they were close.

When they crawled up to the berm Matt got his first view of the dacha. It was in every sense of the word a mansion. Three stories of magnificence. Windows everywhere. Matt murmured at the eight-foot-high fence. The gate operated electronically to allow access. The night lit up like Las Vegas. Three towering light fixtures blasted the site with megawatt power.

"Where are the dogs? I don't see them."

"They let them out at night. They will show up soon. Patrolling all night long."

"How many guards total?"

"Only eight. One who directs the dogs. Two men upstairs protecting Gregor, one man in the back, two men trade off patrolling the fences away from the dogs, two men resting in the barracks from working the day shift. Four dogs."

"Tawnya I'm not embarrassed to say that this scares the shit out of me. How are we going to do this without getting blown away?"

"You asked me once to trust you. Now I ask you to do the same with me. We will be fine. You will see."

"Yeah, that is if I am still alive to use my eyes. Okay what's next?"

"We wait. Maybe two hours. Let the guards become complacent. One more thing I need to confirm."

The summer breeze kept them cool and kept the bugs to a minimum. Soon Matt shuddered a deep gasping breath.

"Oh my God. Look at the size of those dogs. They must weigh over a hundred pounds each."

Four giant hounds loped along the fence, growling at nothing in particular. Just being menacing. Matt's worried expression was plain to see. Then surprise. Good grief, Tawnya's grin was wide and her face showed no fear .

"They could tear us apart so fast we couldn't even scream. Tawnya this is insane."

"When the dogs come out the fence is no longer electric. They do not want to harm the dogs. And they are my friends. When I was living here, I used to play with them at night. I would leave my room and grab treats for them. The one in front is Bear, he is a sweetheart. There is Yeti, Gnome, and Pocomaxa. Is translating to wolverine."

"You think they will remember you? Pardon me, I will not believe that huge animal is a sweetheart."

"Here is plan. I will enter under the fence and lay quietly in the grass. It is tall enough to cover me. When the dogs discover me, I will wait for the guard to investigate and take him out. We then have weapons."

"And me? What do I do?"

"Easy, wait for my signal. Then we go disable the generators. Simple, no?"

"I have a feeling it will be a bit more difficult than

that. I guess I crawl under the fence like you?"

"You have good grasp of this plan. Then we cause havoc. Is my favorite English word. I am good at havoc."

Three times in the last two hours, the four dogs leisurely circled the fence, sniffing, marking territory, investigating interesting smells. The single guard following them smoked two cigarettes and checked where the dogs stopped. Three additional guards circled single file behind the dogs. A gap between the extra guards was roughly ten minutes. Tawnya tapped Matt on the shoulder as a man and four dogs headed around the corner for another lap. Matt checked his watch, 2:15 a.m., and showed it to Tawnya. They waited to allow the two following guards to pass and then Tawnya tapped Matt's shoulder again.

"Is good time to go. Watch where I sneak under the fence. When I take care of guard you follow." She gave him a thumbs up.

"Be careful. I don't want to go home by myself."

A quick run put her at the fence. She bent down, pulled the bottom of the fence up and rolled inside. Hunkered down in the knee-high grass she was invisible. Now to wait for the dogs to arrive. She was glad Gregor's people had not found the place in the fence she had worked on to allow her to escape the confines when she felt like it. Many nights she had run through the forest to release tension and feel somewhat free.

The cool grass refreshed her, and she was thankful the dogs had not found that spot to pee in. Tawnya turned toward the house so she could be ready to tackle the guard. A short time later she heard the hounds. Growls and excited whimpering alerted her that they were close.

Then a huge form towered over her. Spittle leaked

from gigantic jowls and splashed on her chest.

"Bear, you have grown even larger, my baby." Her soft Russian voice halted the growling. An enormous tongue began to lick her face and body, threatening to pull her out of her spot. Three more tongues joined, and the four dogs surrounded Tawnya.

"Here what is going on?" The man tried to pull off one of the dogs to see what they had.

The Ak-74 strapped to the man's back swung wildly as he tugged at Bear's collar. Tawnya grabbed the strap and yanked hard. Swiping her feet into him he dropped to the ground. She used Bear's fur to pull herself up and kicked the guard's jaw. He went slack.

Quickly searching the unconscious man Tawnya recovered a knife, his rifle, two extra magazines, a holster containing a pistol, and a half full bottle of water. She signaled to Matt and then gave all four dogs some love. Matt joined her.

"Good work, Tawnya."

"I give you the pistol, I am happy with the rifle."

"What about the guard?"

"I know this man. Do not worry about him. He is not a nice person." She turned and thrust the knife into the guard's heart. Then dragged his body over to the fence. "We take him to the trees."

Soon they slipped back under the fence, much to the delight of the dogs. Matt let Bear sniff his hand and ruffled the dog's fur to let him know he's a friend. Tawnya gave them a command to continue their patrol. Three of the dogs bounded off but Bear hesitated, whining. She pointed at the retreating dogs and gave the command again. Bear galloped off.

"Generator is this way, that small building over

there." She waved at a shed just inside the fence about fifty yards north.

With the accompanying dogs as cover they hunched over and crouched in front of the padlocked shed door.

"I didn't bring my lock pick. What you got?" Matt held out his hands.

"Better than pick." She bent down on the left side of the door and reached in underneath and pulled out a key. "This. They leave key here to make it easier to enter."

Matt nodded.

The shack was a bit bigger than Matt had thought. The light from outside, which was minimal, revealed a van-sized electrical unit blasting vibrations. Oil and grease smells assailed his nostrils. On the right side of the unit two large generators sat ready to kick in when the power was lost.

"When I shut off power, the generators are supposed to start. I will turn them off also. Then I expect two guards to come investigate the problem. I will take the first with my knife. You can take the other?"

"This pistol is made with metal. I think it will do nicely." Matt waved the barrel toward the door.

"We will each take a side at the door. When the first man opens it, I will bring him in."

"A good plan. You know what they say about good plans?"

"What?"

"There are no good plans. The unexpected always happens."

"After we deal with the guards, I will turn the generators on and give them light again. We will wish for a good outcome. Come we will turn off these noisy machines."

Tawnya pulled the switch and the sudden darkness and quiet hit like waking up from a bad dream. Twenty seconds later the generators kicked on and Tawnya turned them off as well.

Then they squatted on either side of the door waiting. A few minutes later the crunch of footsteps on the gravel outside let them know company had arrived.

As she had said, the first man poked his head inside and he was yanked across the threshold. She buried her knife in basically the same place as before, dead center. Matt swung into the vacated area and brought his pistol barrel hard to the back of the second man's head in a loud crack. He sank to the ground.

Yes, plans have a way of changing. A third man punched Matt's stomach hard with the butt of his rifle. Matt doubled over and tried to gasp in air. He grabbed the rifle and shoved the barrel into his assailant's stomach, careful not to fire the weapon. Both men wheezed and wrestled into a bear hug. The rifle fell to the floor.

Matt remembered his training and with maximum effort raised up to full height slamming his head into the guard's chin. The man's jaw clicked shut and he thought he heard teeth breaking. Tawnya's knife ended the man's life as his eyes went glassy and he leaned to one side. With a shrug of her shoulders, she did the same to the last guard, checking for a pulse in all three. She signaled good to go.

Matt sat on the wooden floor and took deep breaths trying to recover. His ribs screamed when he did. He hoped nothing was broken.

"Are you okay?" Tawnya knelt beside him.

Matt couldn't talk yet, he just nodded. She helped

him up and he gingerly felt around his ribs. Definitely will be bad bruising but he didn't think any were broken. He'd had broken ribs, and this didn't seem as bad. But they really hurt. It would be a while before a painless deep breath could be had.

"Broken ribs?"

He shook his head. "Don't think so. I need a minute though."

"I will turn the generators on."

When she switched on the generators the lights in the house popped on. They searched the bodies and geared up with weapons. Each of them carried a rifle, pistol, and extra ammo. Matt stripped the camouflaged uniform from the first man and put it on over his clothes. The blood smears were not too noticeable. The baseball cap fit snugly on his head. And the sheath and K-bar knife the man carried now nestled at Matt's waist.

Tawnya also donned the uniform of the smaller guard. The blood stain was worse on her blouse. She tucked her hair up under her stolen cap. She found another padlock key and put it in her pocket.

Matt peeked out the shed's door. No one was coming. He took a hurtful breath. They left and closed the door and locked it. Tawnya held up two keys for Matt. One she put back in her pocket and the other she tossed over the fence. Then they headed for the barracks. Four down and four to go.

Chapter 27

Around the back of the house a one-story cabin served as the barracks. They crouched and ran for the north side. Bushes in front and at the side helped cover them as they listened for any sound that would indicate the remaining guards had been alerted to their presence. Nothing so far.

The light breeze would carry sound a good distance at this hour, so they kept silent as much as possible. Six steps led to the cabin porch. Tawnya had said the door is never locked. Why should it be? It's where the KGB contingent lived.

Matt was about to climb the stairs when the door opened. He placed his hand over Tawnya's mouth and pointed to the porch. They eased back farther into the bushes and watched. A match snapped against wood as someone lit a cigarette. The unmistakable sound of a zipper being pulled down and a stream of pee landing on the ground followed. Fortunately, it aimed to the other side of the porch.

They had about two minutes before the next guard came by. Matt watched puffs of smoke arch into the sky. As the man turned to go inside, Matt shot up the stairs and grabbed the man in a choke hold. He jabbed the nice four-inch blade knife of the deceased guard into the man's chest. He died quickly. Matt dragged him down the stairs and into the bushes. They pushed the body under the porch.

As Matt turned to escape from under the porch, a slobbery tongue threatened to rip skin off his jaw. Bear had completed his round and came back to find them.

"Aw, God. Come on dog." Matt wiped his face.

Bear then applied his tongue to Tawnya's face. She fluffed his huge head and again gave him the patrol command. His expression told everyone he was sorely disappointed at having to continue, but he loped off once again protecting the compound from everyone but them.

Matt and Tawnya crept up the stairs of the barracks and stood at the door, knives ready. They quickly entered and disposed of the two snoring men inside.

Both took a breath.

"Now we go deal with Gregor."

"I count at least one more guard inside the house, maybe two. Give me the layout of the house."

"Downstairs, wide lobby has staircase to the left, down hallway on right is library, bathroom, living room, dining room. On left guest room, another guest room, then large kitchen. Upstairs left game room, guest room, exercise room, on right, guest room, guest room, bedroom."

"Where do you think the remaining guards will be?"

"Could be anywhere, even downstairs. They roam at night because of boredom."

"Okay we will need to clear the house before we take care of Gregor."

"We are prepared." Tawnya held up her rifle in her right hand and her knife in the left.

"Let's do it. Quietly if possible." Matt nodded.

Keeping close to the house, they jogged bent over. At the edge of the porch Tawnya held up her hand. She cupped her hand to her ear signaling that she wanted to listen for any sounds. The blazing light revealed no movement. No sound was heard.

Then the dogs spotted them and came running. Tawnya grabbed Bear by the collar and directed him to the dog kennel to the left of the house. The other dogs followed closely.

Tawnya returned and they mounted the steps. She entered a code to shut off the alarm. Matt breathed a sigh of relief that the code had not changed. Inside Tawnya took right and Matt left. Again, they listened. Music played somewhere which would help mask any sound they would make.

Methodically they cleared the main floor. Quiet and void of enemies. They returned down the hall and started up the stairs. Tawnya peered around the corner at the top and motioned for Matt to follow. They cleared all rooms except for one on the left, a game room, and the bedroom on the right.

Music wafted through the open door of the game room. Tawnya quickly looked inside and pulled back.

"Guard is playing a computer game. I will eliminate him," she whispered.

"No. Keep him alive. We can question him. When relief comes and to verify anything Gregor might say."

"Yes, good plan. Be right back." She slid into the room.

"Thunk." Matt moved to the doorway just in time to witness an unconscious guard being eased to the floor. She flashed an okay sign to Matt. He checked his watch. Three thirty. *Not bad for two unarmed people soundlessly wiping out an entire eight-man security team. Certainly glad Tawnya's on my side. What was I worried about?*

Tawnya joined Matt and they both listened at the bedroom door. Heavy snoring threatened to drown out the music. She tried the doorknob and it turned. The door slid smoothly inside, and they ducked down. The form on the bed had not moved.

They approached the immense bed and the AK-74 Tawnya had acquired pointed at Gregor's face. He lay on his back, mouth open and emitting thunder mirroring snorts. She pushed the barrel into his mouth.

The man's eyes popped open, and his eyebrows raised. Recognition flooded his face. He tried to speak but there was no room for his tongue to move. Tawnya leaned over and flicked a bead of his sweat off his nose.

"Gregor, how nice of you to invite me here. Oops I guess that may be a bit presumptuous of me. Did you invite me?"

Her hands did not quaver. Gregor tried to nod his head. He blinked rapidly. She removed the barrel and let him swallow and try to talk. It took him a few seconds to blow out a breath.

"What are you doing here? Why have you not contacted me?" He spat out the words slowly.

"Do you see this rifle? It is significant. I quit. I no longer work for you. Or anyone for that matter. You will no longer be in control. Of anything. What are your last words?"

"You cannot kill me. The KGB will hunt you down. Ungrateful wench."

Tawnya grunted. "Ungrateful? You pig, I did everything you ordered me to do. I did it better than anyone else and what did you do? You sent a team after me. Have you had a report from them lately?"

Gregor's forehead wrinkled.

"What do you want of me? Where are my guards?"

"Your guards are now deserving a fitting burial. And that is what you are facing. All the times you snapped your fingers and caused the death of someone, it was just a business. You convinced yourself that it was for the Motherland." She snapped her fingers. "It is your turn."

"No, please. I can pay you and I swear that no one will come after you. How much will it take? I have enough."

"So, you will not find me and kill me? You swear?"

Gregor's head nodded quickly.

"How about one million US dollars?"

"Agreed. My safe in my office. Let me get to it." He waved a hand toward the door.

"Let's go see." Tawnya motioned with her weapon for him to get out of bed.

Gregor peeled back the covers and twisted to rise. Tawnya stepped back. Matt remained at the door his gun aimed at the man as well.

"Can I get dressed?"

"No. And not shoes either. Barefoot. Walk."

Gregor's checkered pajamas barely covered his immense stomach. He waddled out into the hallway. He stopped when he noticed his guard flat on the floor.

"All dead. No one is coming to your rescue. Continue." Tawnya tapped his back with the gun.

He opened the door of the room next to the game room and they entered. It was spacious and dark. Beside the desk sat a safe the size of a small refrigerator. He turned on a desk lamp and reached for the safe's dial to unlock it.

"Stop. Give Matt the combination. He will open it."

Matt bent down in front of the safe and Gregor recited a series of numbers. There was an audible click and Matt pulled on the door. Inside he reached and showed Tawnya a Russian pistol.

"Always the careful one, eh Gregor? Any money in there, Matt?"

"No. A few rubles but nothing substantial."

"How about a black velvet pouch? Do you see one?" Gregor trembled. "No, Tawnya, no!"

"Yes. It's here." He lifted it up for her.

"This will be my salary. You may look inside."

"Oh my God. Diamonds. Must be a hundred or so."

"Matt did you know that Russia is the world's largest diamond producer? Those are pink diamonds. Very rare. I had to recover them a year or so ago. They were stolen by a rival of Gregor. I believe that since I brought them back, I should claim them."

"Tawnya those are the only ones I have. I can get your money. More than a million. Ten." Gregor's unruly eyebrows furrowed deeply.

"Imbecile. You think I would take your word to hand over money? When does your next team of guards arrive, Gregor?"

"They come at 7:30."

"Perfect. Go sit in your chair."

She watched as Gregor sat. She turned and took the pouch from Matt. I can be a comfortable American with these." She winked at Matt. Then she twirled and let loose a burst from her rifle. Gregor slumped onto his desktop, his hand still in the middle drawer. One bullet in the chest and two in his forehead.

"Gregor always keeps an extra gun in his drawer. You can check if you like."

Matt walked over and peered down at the drawer. As she said his hand was wrapped around a pistol grip. He shook his head.

"Now we go to my room."

"Your room?"

"I lived here for over two years. I should say I was imprisoned here."

They walked the length of the upper hallway and Tawnya stopped at a small bedroom. She pushed open the door and they entered. She pointed to a closet.

"I still have clothes in there." She removed the clothes taken from the guard and replaced her bloody blouse with a fresh one. Then she rummaged inside and pulled out a short black coat. She held it up. "This is the coat I used to bring back the diamonds. The lining is special."

She grabbed the bottom of one side and felt inside. Then she stuffed the pouch in a disguised pocket and shrugged into the coat. She patted the coat.

"Metal detectors do not single out the diamonds." She laughed. "I am one rich woman."

Matt laughed. "Yes, you are. Let's go."

"Wait a minute. One last chore up here." She walked back to the game room and a short burst ensured no witnesses remained. She wiped down the rifle and threw it in the room.

"No witnesses left?" Matt said.

"No, not a one. The way I executed everyone; the authorities will assume this is a fight between oligarchs. We have a couple more tasks to complete. I will bring the vase here and put it on Gregor's desk. It will get to the president. Pietor has returned to his homeland. You can find some clothes to wear in Gregor's room."

"I hope that car you got for us will make it back to our boat. It seemed like it was about to die."

"Not to worry your head. I have other plans for transportation. As soon as I return, we will go. I will let you wait downstairs and relax."

Half an hour later Tawnya carried the vase up to Gregor's office and motioned for Matt to follow. Tawnya carefully set the vase in front of Gregor's still body. Then they descended the stairs.

"We go out the back door. This way."

The kitchen appliances gleamed in the dim lighting. Tawnya reached up and opened a small panel next to the back door. Key fobs hung from ten hooks inside. She selected one and waved to Matt.

Matt watched this woman with awe. She was a one-person hit squad, resource agent, and acted like this was a walk in the park. He wondered briefly why he had worried about coming here, and whether he should have just let her go on her own.

No, he would have missed a myriad of operational miracles, and a mini hurricane of adrenalin blasts such as he hadn't experienced since leaving the service or the ordeal where he lost his fiancé. And this one had to be a classic.

They filed out the back and headed for a garage with six overhead doors. Entering through a side door, Tawnya flipped on the lights. Matt sucked in a breath. A hurtful breath. Off to their right a silver sports car, and a sleek dark blue Italian race car waited to split the air. To the left four black SUVs filled the remaining slots. She pressed the fob in her hand and one of the SUVs flashed lights.

"We don't get to take the race car?" Matt questioned

as he climbed into the passenger seat.

"No, this will do nicely. Buckle up." She started the engine and pushed a button on a pad above her head. The garage door opened, and they screeched out. Another button opened the gate, and they followed the GPS toward the boat dock.

"What about the dogs?" Matt hadn't thought about them in all the commotion.

"They are sleeping in their pen. Plenty of food and water. I said goodbye."

"Oh, the car we came in? We need to dispose of it," Matt added.

"Done. I'm afraid the car has drowned. I drove it off Gregor's dock. I thought about taking his yacht, but it would be very hard to hide such a monster. It is 310 feet long. There it is, off to the west."

"God, I thought that was a military ship."

"Plenty of room. It has a heliport and his own private garden on board. Crew of six."

"You're right. It would be easy to track down and we would be going very slow."

"I must confess. I thought about putting a full mag of bullets into it so it would sink, but it is a beautiful ship. With my salary I think I could buy one of my own." Tawnya giggled. She couldn't ever remember doing that before.

The trip back to the boat they had borrowed seemed anticlimactic. They reached the dock area and parked the big SUV. After wiping down the car to eliminate prints the customs office remained the last possible problem in escaping Russia.

Hefting their single bag of luggage, Matt followed Tawnya inside the office. One customs official sat in a chair puffing on a cigarette. He was not the same agent they had encountered the day before. He looked bored. His wrinkled and loose-fitting customs uniform spoke volumes about him. Someone didn't like him and stuck him in a faraway outpost that seldom offered any excitement.

Tawnya placed her purse on the conveyor belt, threw her coat over her arm and walked up to the metal detector. She grinned at the agent.

He gave her a once over and stood. He motioned her through and busied himself rummaging through the handbag. A thorough search discovered no contraband. Her handed her the purse and waved Matt through. Nothing was found, they had disposed of their weapons in a river they passed on the way to the dock.

He began questioning Matt and Tawnya stepped up.

"He is Canadian and does not speak our language. I will be happy to translate for you." Her flirting smile and batting eyebrows won him over.

"Have you anything to declare?" He grinned.

"Just that Russia has the cutest customs agents." She tilted her head at him.

He blushed deeply and Matt didn't know what the Russian translation for "aw, shucks" was but it definitely implied.

The man uttered a brief statement and indicated they could leave. Once they had gathered the luggage, they left the office. Matt asked Tawnya what the agent had said.

"Your Russian is impeccable, and I wish you a safe voyage, miss." She had half curtsied, and they trotted off to the boat.

Once onboard they relaxed. The cruise to Finland

could be called anticlimactic. The next day they were on a 767 to London, then a flight to New York's LaGuardia Airport where Matt's plane awaited. After two more intermediate stops for sightseeing and recouperation, they arrived back in San Jose.

Epilogue

A Week Later

The technician stood at attention holding the vase. His blood seemed to be heating up and he was sure that his beating heart could be heard out loud. The next few minutes had a direct impact upon how much longer it would continue to pulse. He approached the president and cleared his throat.

"You have completed your analysis?" Malinova's expression soured.

"We have, sir."

"And your conclusion?"

The analyst shifted from one foot to the other and replied. "Mr. President I can say with absolute certainty that these remains are eighty to eighty-five percent confirmed to be from your family. Definitely a child of yours, sir. I am so sorry."

President Malinova sighed and waved the man off. He scurried out the door.

"My daughter is dead." He addressed his second in command, Yuri Polikov. "A man should not live longer than his child. Thank you for bringing this to my attention. Give me the details when you found the vase."

"The KGB leader had not been answering calls for a few hours and when we could not reach anyone at his compound, we sent a team to investigate. They found his entire crew deceased. All knife wounds except for

Baconovic, and two of his guards.

"They had been shot. We believe this may have been a retaliation from a rival oligarch. Gregor had been feuding with two powerful men for some months. We know your daughter had assassinated people in both groups."

"This was a response?"

"Yes, sir. We think so. It has all the earmarks of an attack by a Spetsnaz team. Members of an elite security team being killed by a knife. This is what these kinds of three or four-man teams do. Make it clear that they can thwart a well-armed squad of guards, quietly and efficiently."

"Now I want to be alone." He turned and slowly entered his private library.

At his desk Alexander Malinova stared at the vase containing Tawnya's remains. It seemed so small to contain his daughter. No tears leaked from his eyes. He had followed for years Tawnya's assignments. They were dangerous and life-threatening. But she was so efficient and smart he had never even considered the possibility she would die.

He sighed and lifted his phone. His call to KGB headquarters would initiate a state funeral for its deceased leader. Gregor Baconovic had failed at his most important task in life, the safety and health of the president's children.

But the announcement they would issue that Gregor had died from a brain aneurism, instead of the three neatly placed holes they had discovered in his body, demanded a public ceremony befitting his position.

His death had been inevitable. If he had not been killed by this attack, Alexander would have driven him to a quiet place in the surrounding forest and Igor, his bodyguard, would have directed two nine-millimeter bullets to the back of his head.

A few minutes later plans had been acknowledged. Now what to do with the vase? It did not seem right to just toss it in the trash. Or bury it in some forgotten cemetery plot. It was too morbid to keep it in his office where he would have to look at it every day. No, something else.

A thought came to him. Why not have it displayed in the KGB headquarters with an honor plaque? Just as the Americans did at the CIA in Washington. Yes, a fitting tribute to her dedication and sacrifice.

He leaned back in his chair and lit a Cuban cigar, lost in thoughts of a life taken too soon.

A week later an article in the Wall Street Journal described the funeral of Gregor Baconovic, esteemed head of the KGB. President Malinova stood beside the casket, closed of course, and gave a one-hour eulogy for his alleged best friend. A full military parade had strutted down Moscow's main thoroughfare, complete with a fly-over of Russian fighter jets.

An auburn-haired woman folded the paper and smiled as she sipped from her teacup. Newly styled shoulder-length hair waved in the breeze. The windows in the towering downtown buildings of San Jose, across from the open-air café flashed reflections in the morning sun, and the cloudless sky streaked with pink, and orange seemed unusually bright. People hurried along the sidewalk heading to work, or breakfast. Many holding a cell to their ear or punching a text on the lighted screen.

The still rising sun's rays highlighted her high cheek bones. She swallowed the last bit of tea and relaxed.

Something brightened her features as she stuffed the paper into her new purse. She rose from her chair at the restaurant, smoothing a knee-length, light blue skirt, also a recent purchase. Extracting a shiny-new credit card, she moved to the counter and stood in line to pay for her breakfast.

A young man with a ring in his nose accepted the card and glanced up at the woman.

"How was your breakfast, Miss…" He turned over the card. "Volk?"

"Could not have been better, thank you." She replaced the card in her wallet which she secured in her purse. Did he not realize that in her former country they used nose rings for cows? The spring in her step as she left could not be mistaken. She was ebullient.

Her card identified her as Sonja Volk resident of San Jose, America. She did not care if the world knew of her happiness. It filled her heart to overflowing and if she had been in a place without people she would have shouted. It was all she could do not to go ahead anyway.

Choosing Volk as her name was what Americans called a no-brainer. Throughout her former career as a spy her Russian nickname was Volk, meaning wolf. It only seemed appropriate.

Today beginning a new American life, she had no assignment, no one to answer to, no need to keep looking over her shoulder for threats. She felt somewhat naked absent a weapon. Was this how every American felt? One thing for sure, she could quickly get used to it.

She hummed as she headed to the jewelry store. Another recently acquired habit. She couldn't wait to get a look at the expression on the jeweler's face when she opened the black velvet pouch.

Finally, she was free.

A word about the author…

J. D. Webb, served in the Air Force in Vietnam and the Philippines as a Chinese linguist, as a corporate transportation manager, then shoe repair and sales shop owner, before becoming an author.

An award-winning author of five novels, an anthology, and two short stories. Incredible Witness the anthology was a finalist in the 2023 Killer Nashville Silver Falchion awards. His latest novel Bayou Chase, a thriller, was published in September 2023 by Wild Rose Press. The soon-to-be-published Free To Be Me was chosen as a top Pick at the 2024 Killer Nashville Claymore Awards.

In 2023 Webb was honored to be elected to the Midwest Writer's Workshop Board of Directors.

Thank you for purchasing
this publication of The Wild Rose Press, Inc.

For questions or more information
contact us at
info@thewildrosepress.com.

The Wild Rose Press, Inc.
www.thewildrosepress.com